PONY ON THE PORCH

Mandy looked at Prince. He was breathing easily. He looked as fit as could be. But what if he jumped? Mandy couldn't bear to think about what might happen.

She turned to James, her mind made up. "Will you help me?" she said.

James looked puzzled. "Help you to do what?"

"Steal Prince," said Mandy. "Steal him and hide him until the jumping is over or until Dad gets here."

"Steal him?" James said in a whisper.

Mandy nodded. "Well? What about it? Are you with me?"

Books in the Animal Ark series

PONY on the PORCH

Ben M. Baglio

Illustrations by Shelagh McNicholas

Cover illustration by
Peter Mueller

AN
APPLE
PAPERBACK

SCHOLASTIC INC.
New York Toronto London Auckland Sydney

**Special thanks to C. J. Hall, B.Vet.Med., M.R.C.V.S.,
for reviewing the veterinary information contained in this book.**

ISBN 0-590-18750-3

12   1 2 3/0

Printed in the U.S.A.   40
First Scholastic printing, May 1998

To Helen Magee

One

The little Welsh pony nibbled gently at Mandy's fingers as she fed him the last of the carrots she had brought for him. "There, boy," she said, running her free hand down his silky neck. "Oh, Prince, I'm going to miss you."

"So am I," said Mrs. Jackson. "But there's nothing else we can do now that Jane has gone to live in York. There's nobody to exercise him, and ponies are expensive to keep."

"How is Jane's nursing program going?" asked Mandy. Jane was Mrs. Jackson's daughter. Mrs. Jackson had been a widow for five years, and she and Jane lived at Rose Cottage, just down the road from where Mandy's grandparents lived.

"Oh, Jane has always wanted to be a nurse," Mrs. Jackson said. "She's loving it. But she's worried about Prince. I only hope we can find him a good home."

Mandy looked around the little orchard at the back of Rose Cottage. Prince's stable was a simple lean-to shed in a sheltered corner of the orchard. It smelled of sweet grass and tangy peat moss, and the air blew fresh and clean under the trees. "He couldn't find a better home than this," she said.

"He's always been happy here," said Mrs. Jackson. She lifted a hand and laid it on Prince's gleaming brown coat. "We've had this pony eight years," she said. "It was Jane's tenth birthday present. I remember the day Fred brought him home. You would have thought he had given Jane the moon, she was so pleased." Mrs. Jackson wiped a tear away. "Oh, well," she said. "What has to be done has to be done, I suppose."

Mandy smiled at her although she felt sad, too. "I'm sure you'll find a good home for him, Mrs. Jackson."

"I won't be sending Prince anywhere they can't keep him properly," Mrs. Jackson said. "When I think of all the ribbons he's won at the Welford County Fair. He's a wonderful jumper. Nearly as good as that pony of Barry Prescott's."

"Barry's pony is bigger than Prince," Mandy said. Barry Prescott was the local doctor's son. He had a bay gelding named Star.

Mrs. Jackson was looking at her. "I don't suppose you would want a pony, would you, Mandy? I know you would look after him."

Mandy laughed. "I've got an ark full of animals, Mrs. Jackson. Mom says if we had any more we would sink. But I *will* miss him, won't I, boy?" and she buried her face in Prince's neck.

A voice called from two gardens away. It was Grandma. Mandy had gone over to say goodbye to Grandma and Grandpa. They were going off for two weeks in the sun. Mandy often stopped by to see Prince when she was over at Lilac Cottage, and Jane had often let Mandy groom him and feed him. "That must be Grandma and Grandpa leaving," she said to Mrs. Jackson.

"You go ahead and give them a hug before they go," Mrs. Jackson said. "And tell them I hope they have a good time in Portugal."

"I'll tell them," Mandy said, giving Prince a final pat. "See you soon," she said to the little pony as she left. She waved as she got to the gate at the back of the orchard. Prince was nibbling the grass contentedly. Yes, she would certainly miss him.

"Well, we're all ready," said Grandma as Mandy turned in at the back gate of Lilac Cottage. "Now give me a hug and tell us to have a good time, and see if you can get your grandfather out of his vegetable garden or we'll miss our plane."

Mandy laughed and dragged Grandpa out of his garden.

Grandpa shook his head. "It's the leeks," he said. "I want them perfect for the Welford County Fair."

Grandma sighed. "Now, you know Walter Pickard is going to look after them for you," she said. "They'll still be there in two weeks' time."

Mandy's father appeared at the back door of the cottage. "Any takers for a vacation in Portugal?" he asked his parents. "If you don't feel like it after all, Emily and I could go." He winked at Mandy. Dad was driving Grandma and Grandpa to the airport.

Grandma gave her son a look. "And leave Animal Ark?" she asked. "You wouldn't stop worrying about it, Adam Hope."

Mandy laughed as Dad bundled Grandma and Grandpa into the car and set off. She watched the car disappear down the lane and got on her bike to go home. She wasn't going to the airport. She had a few things to do at home, like check up on a rabbit with an infected paw and pay a visit to a puppy that had been abandoned with a broken leg. Betty Hilder had brought him in, and Mandy had named him Toby. Betty ran the local animal shelter.

She hadn't been joking when she told Mrs. Jackson they had an ark full of animals. They did — Animal Ark, where her mom and dad were vets.

Mandy whizzed down the road, long legs pedaling and thoughts of Toby and Prince filling her mind. She was sure Betty could find a home for Toby with somebody in the village — he was so cute and lovable. But she might only see Prince a few more times before he had to leave Welford.

There was a new girl in Mandy's class. She stood beside Miss Potter. She didn't look very happy. Mandy sighed. She was still thinking about Prince — only now she wondered where he was. She had been so busy these last two weeks she hadn't had time to go over to Rose Cottage until just a few days ago. The stable in the orchard had been empty, and Mrs. Jackson wasn't at home. Mandy had just stood there with the sun dappling the grass at her feet. She had stared at the empty stable for a long time, until her eyes blurred over with tears. Prince was gone.

"This is Susan Collins," Miss Potter was saying. Miss Potter was Mandy's teacher. She was really nice, with flyaway mouse-brown hair and big eyeglasses. Mandy looked at Susan. She wasn't as tall as Mandy and she wasn't as thin either. Her dark hair was drawn back in a ponytail.

That made Mandy think of Prince again. It wasn't so much that he had gone away. After all, she knew he was going. It was not saying good-bye properly that hurt so much. Even her mom and dad hadn't heard where Prince had gone.

"Now," said Miss Potter, "I need somebody to help Susan settle in. Mandy, you could do that."

Kate and Melanie, Mandy's friends, nudged her. "Wake up," said Kate.

"I can find my own way around," Susan was saying. Her accent sounded different. Not like somebody from Yorkshire.

Miss Potter carried on regardless. "Susan comes from London," she said. "So living in the country is going to be a big change for her." She put Susan in the seat beside Mandy. "But I'm sure you will all help her — especially you, Mandy."

As Susan sat down Mandy said, "You'll get used

to it soon. It must be hard coming to a new school."

"I don't want to get used to it," Susan said. "I want to go back to London. London was much better than this."

"Wait and see," Mandy said encouragingly. "You'll like it once you get to know everybody."

Susan tossed her ponytail. "I won't," she said. "I hate it. There's nothing to do."

Mandy thought about all the things she did — especially helping out at Animal Ark. "There's always lots to do in the country," she said. "You'd be surprised."

"Like what?" asked Susan.

"Well," said Mandy, "we have the Welford County Fair on Saturday. That's terrific. There are side-shows and pet shows and equestrian events and . . ."

"Equestrian events?" asked Susan. She looked thoughtful.

"You see," said Mandy. "You'll like living here."

Susan scowled. "I won't," she said as Miss Potter started the lesson. "And you won't make me — not you or anybody else."

Mandy blinked. Susan sounded really determined to hate her new home. She wondered why.

By three-thirty that day Mandy had decided that Susan Collins was a complete pain. At lunchtime, when they were talking about where they lived, she went on and on about the house she lived in.

"It's called The Beeches," Susan said, her nose in the air. "It's the new house on the Welford road. It has a veranda running all the way around the front and stables at the back and a paddock going right down to the road."

Mandy and James passed that way every day biking to school. So that was who had moved into the big new house. "That must be great," she said.

Susan turned to her. "It's a lot better than living in

a cottage," she said. "Imagine living in an ark. I think I'll call you Mrs. Noah."

Then at study hall it had been her computer. "Do you have one, Mrs. Noah?" Susan asked after spending five minutes telling Mandy everything her computer could do.

Mandy shook her head. "No, but James does. He really likes computers."

"James who?" asked Susan.

"James Hunter," Mandy said. "He lives in Welford, too. We bike to school together every day."

"Is he your boyfriend?" asked Susan.

"No," Mandy said, trying to keep her temper. "He's just a friend." Susan really was annoying.

All day long Susan didn't miss a chance to say how much she hated the country. But as she walked Susan to the school gate at three-thirty Mandy got a surprise.

"Isn't there anything you like about being here?" Mandy asked.

Susan looked as if she were going to say no. Then she stopped. "Dad bought me a pony," she said. "I like that."

Mandy's eyes popped. "A pony!" she said. "Can you ride?"

"Of course I can ride," said Susan. "I learned in London. At the best riding school, of course. I did show jumping as well."

Mandy's eyes were shining. "Ponies are wonderful," she said. "You'll have so much fun looking after a pony."

Susan snorted. "The stables looked after the ponies where I learned to ride," she said. "I didn't have to do a thing."

"But didn't you want to do it yourself?" asked Mandy.

"Ugh!" said Susan. "Nasty smelly old straw and mucking out. No, thank you, Mrs. Noah."

"But if you have your own pony . . ." said Mandy.

Susan shrugged. "The gardener looks after it," she said.

Mandy shook her head. How could anyone have a pony and not want to look after it? That was the fun part.

"I couldn't be bothered with all that," Susan said. "I just like riding. My mom is a wonderful rider."

"Does she have a horse, too?" asked Mandy.

Susan looked away. "No," she said. "She lives in London. She has to. She's an actress. She's famous. She's in *Parson's Close*. She plays the pastor's wife."

"My grandmother watches that on TV," said Mandy. "She loves it." Then she stopped. Suddenly

Susan was looking terribly unhappy. "Is that why you want to go back to London?" asked Mandy. "Because your mom's there?"

For a moment she thought Susan was going to answer her. But Susan only laughed and said, "Why would anybody want to stay in a stupid place like this when they could live in London? What is there to do — apart from your stupid Welford County Fair?"

"The Welford County Fair *isn't* stupid," Mandy began.

But Susan wasn't listening. Her eyes lit up. "Maybe if I got her interested in horses again. She used to be interested . . ."

"Hi!" James came up to them, pushing his bike. His straight brown hair was tousled as usual, and his glasses were halfway down his nose.

"This is Susan," said Mandy. "She's new, and her dad's coming to pick her up."

"In his car," Susan said. "It's a sports car."

"Don't you have a bike? Why don't you bike to school like us?" James asked. "It's fun."

Susan put her nose in the air. "Of *course* I have a bike," she said. "A mountain bike. And it's much better than those two."

James looked at Mandy. "Our bikes are okay," he said.

Susan just smiled. "Wait till you see my dad's car," she said. She turned to Mandy. "Is your dad rich?" she asked.

Mandy thought of her dad. Sometimes he treated the animals people brought to him for free. Like Tommy Pickard's hamsters. Tommy was seven and hadn't realized that feeding chewing gum to hamsters wasn't good for them. He came into Animal Ark every day to see how they were doing.

"No, my dad isn't rich," said Mandy, "but the animals are lovely."

Susan looked at her. "I suppose you talk to them," she said.

"Of course," said Mandy. "Animals like being talked to. Don't you talk to your pony?"

Susan tossed her head. "That's different," she said. "I wouldn't talk to hamsters."

"*All* animals like being talked to," said Mandy firmly.

Susan just laughed. "I don't think I'll call you Mrs. Noah anymore," she said. "I think I'll call you Doctor Doolittle. You talk to the animals."

Mandy got really angry then. "It's better than talking to some people," she said.

Just then a big blue sports car pulled up outside the school gates. There was a man in the driver's seat. He leaned over and opened the passenger door. "Hello," he said. "I see you've made friends already, Susan."

Susan's father looked across at Mandy and James.

He was smiling. He had a nice smile but, just the same, he looked as if he was thinking about something else.

"Why don't you ask your new friends to dinner?" he said to Susan. "How about Wednesday? I'll let Mrs. Taylor know." Then he looked at his watch. "Get in, Susan," he said. "I'm in a hurry. I have a meeting to go to."

Susan tossed her hair and made a big thing of getting into the car.

"See you tomorrow," Mandy said as the car took off in a rush.

James turned to Mandy. "What a pain that girl is," he said.

Mandy wheeled her bike out of the gates. "I really tried to be friendly," she said. "But all she does is brag about what she has and how rich they are."

"Forget it," said James. "How are Tommy's hamsters?"

Mandy smiled and shook her head. "Poor things," she said. "Dad had to snip off most of their whiskers and all the fur around their noses and paws. They were covered in the stuff. We're keeping them at the Ark for a few days just to make sure they didn't swallow any of it."

Mandy launched into an update on all of Animal Ark's patients. James had a Labrador retriever named Blackie and a kitten named Eric. He was always interested in hearing about animals.

By the time they got to the Fox and Goose, where the road to Animal Ark branched off, Mandy had nearly forgotten Susan. Nearly, but not quite. At least she hadn't forgotten the pony. They brought their bikes to a halt.

"See you tomorrow," said James.

"Don't forget to tell your mom you're going to dinner at Susan's fancy house on Wednesday," said Mandy.

James pushed his glasses up onto the bridge of his nose and looked at her.

"You don't have to go," he said. "I mean, why punish yourself?"

Mandy bit her lip. "Wouldn't you like to see the pony?" she asked.

James shook his head. "You're impossible!" he said. "You don't even like her."

Mandy grinned. "I know," she said. "But it isn't Susan I'll be going to see — it's the pony."

James grinned back and shook his head. "All right," he said. "I give up. Count me in."

Mandy watched him ride away. James lived at the other end of the village. Mandy wheeled her bike up the path to the old stone cottage. The path up to the red front door ran between banks of flowers, and a wooden sign saying ANIMAL ARK VETERINARY CLINIC swung in the breeze. The veterinary office was a modern building tacked onto the back of the cottage.

The office window was open. Mandy waved to Jean Knox, the receptionist, as she wheeled her bike past.

Jean waved back cheerfully, her glasses dangling on the end of their chain. "Have a good day at school?" Jean called.

Mandy shrugged. "It was all right," she said.

Jean gave her a look but didn't say anything. Simon, the nurse, came to the window. "Never mind," he said. "Everybody has a bad day sometimes. The animals are waiting for you."

Mandy looked at the two faces. "Oh, it wasn't so bad," she said, and Jean smiled.

It was good to be home. Grandma and Grandpa were due back from vacation late tonight. Maybe they would know where Prince was — and Mrs. Jackson. And soon she would go and see Toby — and find out how Tommy's hamsters were doing. And she would talk to them, she thought. No matter what Susan Collins said.

Two

When Mandy woke up next morning the sun was shining through her bedroom window. It was a lovely day. She lay perfectly still for a moment and looked around.

She loved her bedroom. It had a low white-washed ceiling with dark oak beams. The walls were covered with animal posters. And Mom had let her choose her own furniture. There was a pine chest at the foot of the bed and an armoire in the corner under the eaves. And she had a table in the window where she could sit and do her homework, looking out at the garden below.

Then Mandy remembered Susan Collins and

groaned as she got out of bed. "Oh, well," she said to a poster of a baby seal, "at least I'm going to see the pony tomorrow." She ran a brush through her short blonde hair.

"Mandy," called a voice from downstairs. "Are you up yet? Or is that a herd of elephants clumping about in your room?"

Mom. Mandy grinned, got up, and opened her bedroom door. The smell of freshly made toast drifted up the stairs to her. She hung over the banister of the narrow wooden staircase. "Morning, Mom," she called. "I'll be right down."

"Don't bring the elephants," called another voice. Her dad.

She showered and dressed in double-quick time and raced downstairs. "Mmm," she said as she gobbled down toast and homemade marmalade. "This is wonderful."

She looked up at her parents — her adopted parents, really, but it never seemed that way to Mandy. Adam and Emily Hope had adopted her when her birth parents had been killed in a car crash years ago when she was a baby. Adam Hope was dark-haired and jolly and really easygoing. Emily had red curly hair and was the organizer in the family. It was funny. They were both vets but they were so different.

"Grandma and Grandpa got back last night," said Mom.

Mandy spoke through a mouthful of toast. "Did you ask them about Mrs. Jackson? Oh, and did they have a good vacation?"

Dr. Emily Hope laughed. "They had a great time and they said Mrs. Jackson has gone to stay with Jane for a few weeks in York."

"So what about Prince?" asked Mandy. "Is he sold?"

"They don't know," Dr. Emily said. "They found a postcard from Mrs. Jackson waiting for them when they got home. She didn't mention Prince."

Mandy gave a deep sigh. Mom looked up. "What's wrong?" she asked.

Mandy shrugged. "It's nothing," she said. "I wish I knew where Prince had gone."

"Is that all?" asked Mom.

Mandy didn't say anything. "Come on, Mandy," said Dad. "If your mom thinks there's something wrong, you can bet your boots there's something wrong. Out with it."

Mandy looked from one to the other. "It's just this new girl at school," she said.

"What new girl?" asked Dad.

"Susan Collins," said Mom.

Mandy looked at her. "How do you know about her?" she asked.

Dr. Emily laughed. "From Mrs. McFarlane at the post office," she said. "Honestly, if a mouse sneezes that woman hears about it."

"Does this Susan have a mouse with a cold, then?" asked Dad. Dr. Emily gave him a look. "Isn't it time you went to work?" she asked.

Dr. Adam Hope grinned and got up from the table. "Okay, I can take a hint," he said as he disappeared out of the kitchen door.

"So what's the problem with Susan Collins?" Dr. Emily asked.

Mandy looked at her mom. She had green eyes and freckles and the kind of smile that made you want to tell her everything.

"Miss Potter asked me to look after her because she's new, but she's horrible, Mom."

Her mom nodded and poured out another glass of juice for both of them. "You've only just met her," she said.

Mandy shrugged. "She says I'm crazy because I talk to animals. She calls me Doctor Doolittle."

Dr. Emily was smiling.

"What are you laughing at?" asked Mandy. "It isn't funny."

"I'm not laughing," said her mom. "I'm just smiling because I remember what it used to be like. And it wasn't funny for me, either."

Mandy's eyes opened wide. "You mean people used to say things like that to you?" she said. Her mom nodded, and Mandy smiled. It made her feel a lot better. "Anyway, James and I are going to her house for dinner tomorrow. Is that all right?"

Dr. Emily nodded. "Of course it is. But why on earth are you and James going if you don't like her?"

Mandy's eyes slid away from her mother's. "Um, well, she has this pony . . ." she began sheepishly.

"You're a disgrace, Mandy Hope," Dr. Emily said with a laugh.

"I don't think Susan wants us to come," said Mandy. "It was her dad who invited us."

There was a sound of gravel spurting outside and a bicycle bell pinged. "That must be James," Mandy said. "I'd better go." She got up from the table and grabbed her backpack. She was at the door when her mother spoke.

"Mandy," she said.

Mandy turned. "Mmm?" she said.

"This girl Susan," Dr. Emily said. "She's just moved here. Maybe she's lonely. There's only her and her dad at that big house, and her dad is too

busy working to have much time for her. He's setting up that new building project on the other side
of Walton."

Mandy nodded. "I know. Her dad is really rich,
according to Susan, and her mom's a famous actress."

Dr. Emily smiled. "She's in one of the soaps
Grandma watches," she said. "Grandma wrote to
her before she went away to ask her to give out the
prizes at the Welford County Fair."

Mandy groaned. "Susan's bad enough as it is. Just
think what she'll be like if her mom's doing the
prize giving. Has she said she'll do it?"

Dr. Emily started clearing the table. "Grandma's
waiting for an answer." Grandma was chairperson
of the Welford Women's Club.

Suddenly Mandy grinned. "What about Mrs. Ponsonby?" she asked. "She always does the prize giving."

Mrs. Ponsonby was a leading light in the
Women's Club. She was really bossy. She lived in
creepy old Bleakfell Hall and had a fat Pekingese
named Pandora.

"Let's put it this way," said Dr. Emily. "I wouldn't
like to be the one to tell Mrs. Ponsonby her services
won't be required."

Mandy shrugged. "She deserves to be taken

down a peg or two," she said. "And she overfeeds that poor little Peke of hers dreadfully."

The bicycle bell pinged again, and Mandy jumped. "I'd better go."

"Now, remember," said Dr. Emily, "Try to make friends with Susan."

Mandy opened her mouth to protest, but she changed her mind. She had to admit that it must be difficult for Susan not to have her mom around all the time. "Okay, Mom," she said. "I'll try, but I don't think it'll do any good."

James popped his head around the kitchen door. "Are you coming?" he asked Mandy. "Hello, Dr. Hope."

"Good morning, James," said Dr. Emily. "How's Eric?"

"He's a holy terror," said James, grinning. "He's driving my mother crazy."

"Huh," said Mandy. "Your mom loves that kitten."

James grinned again. "So does Blackie," he said. "Come on. We'll be late if we don't hurry."

Mandy and James pedaled up the hill that led out of Welford. As they passed the church, Mandy caught sight of a familiar figure in the field behind. She slowed her bike and stopped by the stone wall that ran around the field. "Hi, Grandpa," she called excitedly. "How was the vacation?"

Grandpa looked up from a post he was hammering into the ground. "Mandy," he said and started to walk toward them. "We had a great time. And best of all, my leeks survived."

"Hi, Mr. Hope," said James. "Getting things ready for the show?"

Grandpa nodded and passed a hand over his brow. "It's hard work for an old man like me. What we need is some young blood."

Mandy laughed. Her grandfather might be retired now, but he was as fit as a fiddle — and really tanned after two weeks in the sun.

"You're young blood compared to some of us," said a voice, and old Walter Pickard appeared around the corner of the churchyard. Walter had once been the local butcher, but he had been retired a long time now. He was a lot older than Mandy's grandfather but he was still spry. "How're those hamsters of our Joe's boy getting on?" he said to Mandy.

Tommy was Walter's great-grandson and the apple of his eye.

Mandy laughed. "They're recovering," she said. "Dad says we'll keep them until the fair — just in case."

"What are you doing?" asked James.

Grandpa laid down his mallet. "Trying to get the jumps figured out for the pony trials," he said.

"Yes," said Walter. "We want to make sure they're suitable. We need somebody to try them out. Usually Barry Prescott does it, but Star is getting over a sprained tendon and he doesn't want to risk it just yet."

"We know somebody with a pony," said James. "We could ask her."

"Susan?" said Mandy, her eyes widening.

"Bring her along on Thursday," said Grandpa. "They should be ready by then."

James was hanging over the wall. "If you need help, we could come over, too," he said.

"Good for you," said Walter. He looked at his watch. "Don't be late for school now."

"Yikes!" said James. "Come on, Mandy. We might just make it."

They pedaled hard to make up for lost time, and they were well out on the Walton road before they slowed down a little. Mandy was enjoying the sun on her back and the breeze on her cheeks. Suddenly it was a lovely morning again. She said so to James and he grinned.

"Was something wrong?" he asked.

Mandy made a face. "Only Susan Collins," she said.

"You should try to ignore her," said James.

Mandy looked at him. "Mom says I should try to make friends with her."

"Friends?" said James.

And Mandy laughed at the expression on his face. "That's how I feel," she said. "But I'll try for Mom's sake."

They passed the big new house where Susan lived. It had lawns and a paddock in front, and Mandy could just catch a glimpse of stables at the back. There was no pony in the paddock.

"Imagine living in that," said James.

Mandy looked at it. "I would rather live in our cottage than that," she said.

"You would rather live in your cottage than any-where else in the world," said James.

Mandy smiled at him. "You're right. I would."

She pedaled faster and lifted her face to the clear country air and the sun. The fields were green with new corn and on the low hills in the distance she could see this year's lambs picking their way among the clumps of grass. Dad said it had been a good year for lambing. Mandy sometimes wished the tiny little lambs didn't grow up so quickly, but Dad only laughed at her when she said that.

"Look at you," he said. "You wouldn't want to stay the same forever, would you?"

But sometimes Mandy thought it would be nice to stay the same forever — if it meant staying in Welford at Animal Ark and looking after animals. But nothing stayed the same forever. Even the animals moved on, like Prince going to a new home. She was sure she would be happy if only she knew he was safe and well with people who would love him and look after him.

Three

They were only five minutes late, and Miss Potter was really good about it when Mandy told her why. "Tell your grandfather if he needs any help selling tickets at the gate or anything like that then I'll be happy to do it," she said.

"Thanks, Miss Potter," Mandy said. It was wonderful how people got involved in the Welford County Fair.

Susan and Mandy were in different classes for most subjects so they didn't see much of each other in school. Mandy asked her to join Melanie and Kate and herself for lunch.

"I've already found a place," said Susan shortly. Then she turned back. "Oh, by the way, Mrs. Taylor says come at six tomorrow night."

Mandy didn't even get a chance to ask who Mrs. Taylor was.

"Don't bother about her," said Melanie after Susan walked away.

"She's a pain," said Kate. "Good riddance."

Mandy sighed. "Maybe she's just homesick," she said, but Kate and Melanie didn't seem to think so.

Just then Barry Prescott stopped by their table. "That liniment your dad gave me really worked," he said to Mandy.

Mandy smiled. "Oh, I'm glad, I'll tell him. Will Star be all right for the show, then?"

Barry nodded. "No problem," he said. "We should win the jumping again."

"Barry always wins," said Melanie as Barry moved on.

"James is entering Blackie in the pet show," said Mandy. "He's been teaching him tricks."

"Blackie?" asked Kate. "I've seen some of Blackie's tricks." Blackie wasn't exactly known for his obedience, but James loved him anyway.

"Like the time he ran away with the field hockey ball at the interschools final," said Melanie.

They all giggled. "I don't think James has been allowed to bring him to any kind of school match since," said Mandy.

"That dog's a dangerous animal," said Kate, and they laughed.

On the way home from school Mandy saw a brown pony at the far end of The Beeches' paddock. It looked so like Prince her heart skipped a beat. Talk about wishful thinking.

"How are Blackie's tricks coming along?" she asked James to take her mind off Prince.

"I'm teaching him to fetch things," James said.

"Is it working?" asked Mandy.

James grinned. "Not really. He fetches things, all right. They just aren't the things you want him to fetch. You should have heard Mom the other day. Blackie came downstairs with a pillow."

"And?" asked Mandy.

"He started to chew it," James said. "There were feathers everywhere, and Blackie chasing them. Every time he sees a feather now he goes for it. He even recognizes the word because Mom was storming around the house shouting 'feathers, *feathers*, FEATHERS.'"

James was coming over to Animal Ark. They went inside, still laughing about Blackie.

"What's got into you two?" asked Jean from her desk as they passed by.

"Feathers," they both said, and she shook her head in despair at them.

Just then there was the sound of car wheels on gravel. Mandy and James turned to the door as it flew open. It was little Penny Hapwell from Twyford Farm. Her mother was carrying a small furry bundle wrapped in a towel — Cally, Penny's kitten. Blood was soaking through the towel, and the kitten's eyes were closed. Mandy's heart turned over as she looked at Mrs. Hapwell's shocked face.

"She isn't dead, is she?" Mandy asked but, looking at the little scrap of tortoiseshell fur, it was hard to believe Cally could still be alive.

At once Jean sprang into action. She rang a buzzer on her desk, and Simon came in immediately.

He took one look at the scene and tapped on the treatment room door. Dr. Adam appeared, took in the situation at a glance, and gently patted Penny's head. "My, my," he said. "Cally has had an accident, has she? Well, don't you worry, okay?"

The little girl looked up at him, her eyes big with tears. "You'll make her better, Dr. Hope, won't you?" she said. "Mommy says you'll make her better."

Dr. Adam smiled at the little girl, but Mandy saw the urgent look he gave Simon. Simon lifted the blood-soaked bundle out of Mrs. Hapwell's hands and carried it into the treatment room.

Dr. Adam turned to Mandy. "Will you look after Penny while I have a word with Mrs. Hapwell?"

Mandy nodded. She couldn't trust herself to speak. She could see how serious the situation was.

Jean looked at Mandy and lowered her voice. "Now, you go and get that little girl some milk and cookies and don't go upsetting yourself," she said. "You know if anybody can save that little kitten, your dad can."

Mandy nodded dumbly. She felt sick to the pit of her stomach. Poor little kitten. Poor Penny. Mandy remembered well the little girl bringing the kitten in for her injections not long after Cally was born.

"Come on, Mandy," said James. "We'll hear soon enough."

Mandy nodded. She was at the connecting door between the house and the office when she asked Jean, "Where's Mom?"

"Over at Baildon," Jean said. "Nothing terrible. Just a horse needing a once-over before he's sold."

Mandy nodded again and let James push her gently through the door into the house. She poured milk and put out a plate of cookies for Penny, who couldn't eat anything. All Mandy could think of was what was going on next door.

"Why don't we take Penny to see the animals in the kennel?" James asked.

Mandy nodded. "Would you like that, Penny?"

The little girl thought for a moment. "Has your daddy made Cally better yet?" she asked.

Mandy bit her lip. "Not yet," she said. "But he will."

Penny nodded solemnly. "I know," she said. "Mommy says so."

They were in the kennel when Mrs. Hapwell came in. "Jean and I think it's best if we go home," she said. "She'll call when she has news."

"Is it going well?" Mandy asked.

Mrs. Hapwell shrugged. "I was only in there long enough to tell him what happened. I've been talking to Jean." She looked at Penny. "Come on, sweetheart," she said. "Let's go home."

"I want Cally," said Penny, starting to cry again.

Mrs. Hapwell bent down and gave her a hug. "We have to leave Cally here for a little while," she said. "Until she gets better."

Penny nodded. "Just till she gets better," she said.

Mrs. Hapwell looked at Mandy over her daughter's head, and Mandy knew at once why she was taking her home. If Cally didn't get better, it would be easier if Penny was at home.

After they had gone Mandy looked at Toby. Dad had set his broken leg with a special plastic bandage called a vet cast. It was much lighter than a plaster one and much better — especially for a puppy.

Toby pushed his little wet nose up against the bars of his cage, and Mandy reached in and picked him up. Cuddling him made her feel a lot better. At last she couldn't stand the suspense about Cally any longer.

"I'm going through," she said to James.

She put Toby back in his cage and gave him a final pat just as the treatment room door opened and her dad stood there, white-coated and masked. There was a smear of blood on the apron he wore over his lab coat.

Mandy's eyes met his and her heart turned over. Then he reached up and drew down the mask that covered his face — and smiled. He looked past her and said to Jean, "Call the Hapwells and tell them everything's going to be all right." Then he turned to Mandy. "I suppose you'll want to see the patient," he said.

Mandy nodded, unable to speak. She followed her father into the treatment room. Simon was laying the little patient gently on a bed of clean muslin. Cally was curled up and fast asleep. Both front paws and one hind leg were bandaged, and there was a light wadding of bandage around her tummy. Mandy stood looking down at the frail little bundle of life. She brushed her tears away and turned to her dad.

"What happened?" she asked.

Dr. Adam scratched his head. "Take one sharp piece of machinery and add one very adventurous kitten," he said, "That's all, just an accident."

"But she'll be okay?"

"Cally?" said Dr. Adam. "Oh, she'll be fine. It looked a lot worse than it was. The biggest concern was that there wasn't much time. I think we'll keep her here overnight. She can go into the residential unit tomorrow if she's well enough."

Mandy looked at her dad. It was at times like these that she knew that all she ever wanted to do was look after animals — maybe even be a vet like Mom and Dad.

Later that evening Mandy talked to Grandpa about it as she helped him stack hay bales for the vegetable stalls. "I don't see why you couldn't be a vet," Grandpa said, "if you work hard enough. It isn't an easy job, you know, not counting all that studying at college."

"I know that," said Mandy, "but it's worth it, isn't it, Grandpa?" She sneezed as a handful of hay came loose and tickled her nose.

Grandpa chuckled. "How would you like to have to look after a great big guy like that?" he said. Mandy looked where he was pointing. A big, powerful workhorse. It was pulling an enormous cartload of fence posts and canvas across the field.

"Yes, Dan," Grandpa called to the man at the leading rein. "Duke's a wonderful sight."

Dan Venables waved but kept on going. "I won't stop, Tom," he said. "You know Duke can't stand being near hay."

Mandy looked at the huge workhorse with its great shaggy mane and bushy tail. Its hooves were enormous. Dan kept Duke's brasses and leathers shining, and Duke had center stage at every Welford County Fair.

Grandpa shook his head. "Funny, a great big horse like that, but put him near hay and he starts wheezing like my old dad's bellows. They used to call it the heaves when I was a boy around my dad's forge." Grandpa's father had been the village blacksmith.

Mandy forked up a drifting pile of hay and stuffed it back under the baling twine. Golden dust danced in the evening light. "That's it," said Grandpa. "That dust. It gets into a horse's lungs. Duke got shut in a hay barn once. It was very serious. That's why Dan is so careful now. Some horses just don't like hay. Most of them aren't bothered."

Mandy patted the hay bales. "The vegetables will look great on here," she said. "Especially your leeks, Grandpa."

Grandpa chuckled. "I would say my leeks are the best in the county," he said. "Not wanting to boast, of course."

Mandy laughed. "Of course not." It was nice to have Grandpa home again.

Four

By the time Mandy got home from school the next day, Cally the kitten was looking much better. Dad allowed Mandy to carry her carefully into the veterinary office. The little bundle mewed piteously up at Mandy, and the kitten's tiny pink tongue rasped gently on her hand.

"There," she murmured to Cally as she laid her very gently on the bottom of an empty cage next to Toby's. "You're going to be just fine."

Dad smiled. "Cally'll be as fit as a flea in a few days. Just wait and see. The younger they are, the better they recover."

Mandy pushed a finger through Toby's cage and tickled his chin. The little dog barked happily. "You have company," she said. "Look after Cally for us."

Toby barked again and licked Mandy's hand. Then he limped over to the end of his cage and snuffled. The kitten looked at him sleepily and blinked. From far down in her tummy came a rumbling noise. She was purring.

"See," said Dr. Adam, "they've made friends." He looked at his watch. "Isn't it time you did some homework if you're going out for dinner?"

Mandy groaned. But then she remembered what Grandpa had said. If she wanted to be a vet, she would have to work hard.

She met James outside the Fox and Goose. She was still unsure about having dinner with Susan. She hadn't been any friendlier today than she had yesterday. "Quarter to six," he said as she skidded her bike to a standstill. "We'll make it easily."

They got to The Beeches just before six. The nearer they got to the house the bigger it seemed to get. "Wow!" said James. "What a place."

"Imagine wanting to live in London when you could live in there," said Mandy. "I think Susan's mom is nuts."

They turned their bikes into a courtyard at the

front of the house. The house was built like a ranch, with a veranda running around three sides of a courtyard. Its windows gleamed in the sun.

They got off their bikes and walked up the steps that led to the veranda. Mandy rang the front doorbell. A woman with a very stern face answered. "I'm Mrs. Taylor," she said. "Susan is out riding. She should be back soon. Come in, but wipe your feet first."

James looked scared to death, and Mandy didn't blame him. The front door was wide-open and she could see inside the house. The hall was floored with gleaming honey-colored wood, and the walls were sparkling white. At one end a big open staircase led to the upper floor.

The place was huge. Even the moving boxes piled neatly at one side of the hall looked impressive. But the house looked cold, too. Mandy thought of Animal Ark and the cozy living room with its red rugs and log fire. She shivered slightly. Maybe once Susan's family finished moving in, The Beeches would look more welcoming.

She rubbed her hands on her jeans in case they were dirty and stepped forward. Just then there was the sound of hooves and Mandy swung around. It was Susan — on her pony.

Mandy couldn't believe her eyes. Then she ran

down the steps of the veranda and threw her arms around the pony's neck. It hadn't been wishful thinking. It really had been Prince she had glimpsed in the paddock yesterday.

"It *is* you," she said, nuzzling Prince's neck. "It's really you. This is where you went. Oh, I've missed you so much." She looked up at Susan, her eyes shining. "I didn't know you had bought Prince," she said. "He's a wonderful pony."

"You mean you know him?" asked Susan. She didn't look too pleased.

Mandy nodded. "Prince and I have known each other for years, haven't we, boy?" Prince whinnied and rubbed his head against Mandy's shoulder. "I was wondering who Mrs. Jackson had sold him to. I'm so glad he hasn't gone far away. Now I'll be able to come and visit him — that's if you'll let me. Oh, isn't he beautiful?" She stopped.

Susan was looking down at her, her face stiff. "Yes, he is," she said sharply. "And he's mine."

Mandy felt as if somebody had thrown a bucket of cold water over her. What on earth had she said?

Susan dismounted, and Mandy held the pony's head. She ran her hand over his flanks. They were steaming a little and damp to the touch. "You'll have to rub him down," she said. "Jane always did after a ride. We used to —"

Susan looked at her. "I don't care what you used to do," she said. "He's *my* pony now. Not Jane's. Just because you know him already doesn't give you the right to tell me how to look after him. I don't need you to tell me what to do."

Mandy looked up. "I didn't mean . . ." she stammered. "Only he's hot."

"Jim will see to him," said Susan. "Won't he, Mrs. Taylor?"

Mrs. Taylor sniffed. "If I can find him," she said.

Mandy remembered Susan telling her the gardener looked after her pony. That must be Jim. "I can do it," she said. "I've rubbed Prince down lots of times. Jane showed me how. Please let me."

Susan scowled. "Jim will do it," she said. "And anyway dinner is ready, isn't it, Mrs. Taylor?"

"I'm just about to put it on the table," said Mrs. Taylor.

"Come on, then," said Susan.

Mandy gave Prince a last pat. "See you later, boy," she whispered. Prince whinnied as Mandy followed Susan into the house. She hated leaving him so soon after finding him again.

Once inside, Mandy looked around. Through double doors at the side of the hall she caught a glimpse of heavy black-and-chrome dining-room furniture. It looked very fancy, but not very welcoming. There was a pile of moving boxes in there, too.

"We aren't having dinner in there, are we?" James whispered in her ear.

"I hope not," Mandy whispered back.

"Of course we haven't gotten everything figured out yet," Susan said, looking around the hall. "Daddy is going to have interior decorators up from London."

"That'll be nice," Mandy said weakly. Interior decorators. She and Mom and Dad had fun painting and wallpapering the cottage when it needed it. Mandy was glad when Mrs. Taylor took them down a passage behind the stairs and through a door at the back into the kitchen. She felt more at home there.

Dinner was really good — scrambled eggs and grilled tomatoes with lots of crusty bread and homemade cookies to follow. Mrs. Taylor could certainly cook.

"That was great," Mandy said when they had finished.

"What do you want to do now?" Susan asked.

"Let's go and see Prince," Mandy said.

Susan frowned. "You've seen him already." She

turned to James, "How would you like to see my new computer?"

James's face lit up. He really liked computers. Mandy sighed. Oh, well, she would see Prince again later.

They went up to Susan's bedroom. It was enormous. It had built-in furniture and a thick new-smelling carpet, but the walls were bare. No posters or pictures.

But her computer was terrific — or so James said. Mandy wasn't very interested in computers. She wandered over to the window that looked out onto the courtyard and frowned. Prince was still there. It was very bad for him to be left sweating after a ride. She looked toward Susan. No use telling her. She would only tell Mandy to mind her own business.

As quietly as she could, Mandy slipped out of the room. It wasn't hard. James and Susan were too involved with the computer to notice her.

She ran downstairs. At the bottom she hesitated, then made up her mind. She turned and made for the door to the kitchen. Mrs. Taylor was busy at the oven. She looked up as Mandy came in.

"Mrs. Taylor," said Mandy. "I'm just going to take Prince around to the stables and rub him down, if that's all right."

Mrs. Taylor looked at her and tut-tutted. "Is that pony still out there?" she asked. "I completely forgot about him. I meant to go and get Jim after I'd given you dinner, but this newfangled stove started acting up, as if I don't have enough to do. You go ahead, dear, and rub him down. Susan says he's already got a cold."

"A cold?" Mandy asked.

Mrs. Taylor removed a cake from the oven and set it on a counter. "Susan says he coughs," she said. "But I don't know anything about horses and neither does Jim. It's surprising Susan took the pony out today at all. She's been keeping him warm in the stable these last few days. I suppose he's company for her. I think she misses her mother. And I don't have time for her. It's as much as I can do to keep on top of the work in a big place like this. You go on and see to the pony."

Mandy ran back through the hall and out into the courtyard. A cool breeze had picked up. Gently she reached up and felt the pony's coat. Still damp, and cold now.

"Come on, boy," she said, taking hold of his reins. "Come on." And she led him around the back of the house to the stables.

The stables were perfect. Everything you could possibly need for looking after a pony was there —

currycombs and hay and water and pitchforks for turning over his bedding of straw. And the whole place smelled of fresh paint and newly cut wood. The stables were so new there were still piles of fine sawdust lying around.

"Not like your old stable, boy," Mandy said. "You've come up in the world." But as she looked around the new stables she wondered if Prince missed the old lean-to in Mrs. Jackson's orchard, the breeze rustling the trees, and the smell of sweet grass.

Quickly she unsaddled the pony and hung up the tack on its hooks. Then she got busy wiping him down, drying him off, and finally giving his coat a really brisk brush.

"There," she said when she had finished. "That's better."

She gave him a pat. He seemed warm again. She hoped he hadn't gotten a chill. Once or twice he coughed. It worried Mandy. Prince had never been ill in his life. But it was warm in the stable and very dry. He wouldn't be chilled.

Mandy talked to the pony as she tidied up. Dust motes from the hay danced in the sunlight coming in through the open stable door.

Just then a man came in. He was wearing boots and carried a ball of twine and a rake. "I thought I heard something," he said. He looked at the pony. "Nobody told me he was back."

Mandy smiled. "You must be Jim," she said. "It's all right. I've got him rubbed down. But he was out in the courtyard a long time. I hope he didn't get chilled."

Jim shook his head. "Nobody told me he was there," he said. "I usually put him right in the stable when Susan has finished riding him."

Mandy smiled. "And out in the paddock on nice days?" she asked.

Jim shook his head. "She won't allow that," he said. "That pony's like gold to her. It has to be in the stable warm and dry all the time."

Mandy looked at Prince. "He was coughing," she said.

The gardener shook his head. "Susan says he has a cold. I don't know much about horses," he said. "But there's been a lot of new paint around this place, and new paint always gives me a cold. So maybe horses are the same. I look after the gardens. I tell you, it's too much — gardens and a pony."

Poor Prince, thought Mandy. Jim was too busy to have much time for him. And poor Susan. Mrs. Taylor was too busy to have much time for *her.*

"I think he's all right now," Mandy said. "But I don't think you should water him for a while, not till he's really warmed up. It might chill him."

"Little Miss Know-it-all," said a voice from the door. It was Susan. "Mrs. Taylor told me you would be here. I told you, he's my pony. You've no right to be here without my permission."

"I was only rubbing him down," said Mandy. "Mrs. Taylor says he has a cold."

Susan frowned. "It's only a little cold, and he was fine when I had him out this afternoon. He didn't cough once."

Mandy tried again. "Prince has always been so healthy. It isn't like him. If you want, Dad can come and look at him. Or you could bring Prince over to Animal Ark."

Susan frowned. "What a fuss. Don't tell me what to do with my own pony," she said. "He's mine, not yours. Just because you knew him before I did doesn't mean you own him. He's mine."

Mandy felt her face go red. That was so unfair. Just then James appeared in the stable door. "Maybe we should go," he said when he saw Mandy's face.

Mandy dragged her eyes away from Susan. How could she be so possessive about an animal? Animals weren't toys or objects. They were real living creatures with personalities.

"Okay," she said to James. As she passed Susan she said carefully, "Look, Susan, I was only trying to help. It's just that Prince isn't a bike or a pair of jeans or . . . or a computer, you know. You can't own animals the way you own things. It just isn't like that."

Susan didn't say anything, but she moved past Mandy and went to stand beside her pony.

Mandy gave up. "Tell Mrs. Taylor dinner was really nice and thank you for asking us," she said. "Oh, I nearly forgot. Would you like to bring Prince over tomorrow to try the jumps for the pony trials at the Welford County Fair? They need somebody to pace them out to make sure they have the distances right."

Susan moved toward the pony and put her arms around his neck. "I might," she said.

Mandy looked at her. Why was she so difficult? "Oh, well," she said. "If you want to help we'll be there around seven."

Susan buried her head in the pony's neck. Her hair was almost the same color as Prince's mane. Then she took a carrot out of her pocket and offered it to Prince.

No, thought Mandy as she looked at Prince's soft

brown mane, his gentle eyes. You didn't "own" animals. Animals weren't things.

The pony whinnied softly and daintily lifted the carrot from Susan's palm with velvety lips. There wasn't a computer in the world that could do that.

Five

Mandy and James went straight to the office at Animal Ark. Jean was just leaving. "That little kitten's perked up amazingly," she said. "She's been trying to get her bandages off."

Mandy laughed. "That's a good sign," she said.

"And Tommy Pickard is in to see his hamsters," said Jean. "That little boy sure misses them terribly."

"Any new animals tonight?" asked James.

Jean hunted around for her car keys and found them in her coat pocket. "A budgie with an impacted crop, but your mom saw to that, Mandy. And Mrs. Ponsonby was in with Pandora."

Mandy groaned. "That poor little dog. She's so fat she can hardly move."

Jean nodded. "Your mom told her that. Mrs. Ponsonby wasn't pleased."

Mandy grinned. "Good for Mom," she said. "I hope she gave her a good talking-to."

"Oh, I did," said a voice from the office door. Mandy turned to see her mother standing there smiling, her red hair tied back from her face. "Not that it'll do any good."

"Mom," said Mandy, "do you think there are people who shouldn't have pets?"

Dr. Emily looked at her. "Mrs. Ponsonby is really fond of Pandora," she said. "If anything really bad happened to that little dog she would be devastated." She sighed. "Still, I wish I could persuade her to keep to a sensible diet."

"Who?" asked James, grinning. "Mrs. Ponsonby or Pandora?"

Dr. Emily laughed in spite of trying to look disapproving. Mrs. Ponsonby was a very large lady.

"Oh, Mom," said Mandy. "You'll never guess. Susan's pony is Prince."

"Prince!" said Dr. Emily. "You've found him. Oh, Mandy, that's great."

The telephone rang. Jean picked it up and spoke

for a moment before handing it over to Dr. Emily. "Calving," she whispered.

Dr. Emily spoke into the receiver. Mandy looked at her — suddenly all brisk efficiency and understanding. "I'll be right there," she said. "Keep her warm and as quiet as possible. I'm on my way."

"What is it?" asked Mandy as her mother put the phone down.

"Baildon Farm," said Dr. Emily. "One of their Jersey heifers. She's very small, and it's her first calf." She looked at the two upturned, eager faces. "Want to come?"

"Yes, please." James and Mandy nodded eagerly.

"You haven't promised to help Grandpa tonight, have you?"

James grinned. "We have the night off," he said.

Dr. Emily smiled. "Okay," she said. "James, you call home to let them know where you are. I'll get my bag, and, Mandy, tell Dad where I'm going. Be at the car in two minutes flat."

They raced to do as they were told. Mandy popped her head around the treatment room door. Dad was there with Walter Pickard and Tommy. The three hamsters were looking slightly bald but were lively enough to run up and down Tommy's sleeve.

"We'll keep them here a little longer," Dr. Adam

was saying. "Just to make sure they haven't swallowed any of that stuff. And remember, Tommy, just because you like chewing gum doesn't make it good for hamsters." The little boy nodded solemnly up at him, his eyes round, his mop of white blond hair dancing with every nod.

Dr. Adam looked up. "How was the pony?" he asked Mandy.

"You'll never believe this, Dad. It was Prince." She laughed at her father's surprise. "I was surprised, too," she said. "Isn't it wonderful? The only thing is, he had a cough. But Susan thinks it's just a cold, and the gardener says new paint gives him a cold, too."

"Probably is," said Dr. Adam. "Paint does that sometimes. But if she's worried, tell her I'll go and see him."

Mandy began to say "I did," but Walter asked, "Is that the girl who's coming to try our jumps?"

Mandy nodded. "At least, she might," she said. Just then she heard her mother's voice in Reception. "James and I are going to a calving with Mom," she said. "Up at Baildon."

Dad nodded. "Molly, a Jersey heifer," he said. "One of your mom's favorites. She delivered that little heifer. Saved her life. Emily's always had a soft spot for her. Now don't get in the way."

"We won't," said Mandy. A car horn honked. "Got to go."

Baildon Farm was high up on the meadow. Mandy had been there a couple of times, and it always seemed as if it were perched on the roof of the world. Mandy loved Baildon. From there you could look down on Welford and Walton sitting like toy villages far below.

Jack Mabson, the farmer, met them at the cowshed door. He looked worried. "She's started, but she's so small . . ." he said to Dr. Emily. He was a big man, but somehow he looked smaller than Mandy's mom just then.

Dr. Emily gave him a reassuring pat on the arm. "She's a fighter, Jack," she said. "She wouldn't be here now if she wasn't. We both know that." She turned to Mandy and James. "Besides, I've brought her some visitors. We can't disappoint them."

Mandy was staring at the cowshed. From inside she heard a faint lowing sound. "Mom . . ." she began, but Dr. Emily was getting her bag, taking out the calving gown, and getting into it. Its rubbery folds covered her from head to toe.

"Water, soap, towels?" she asked Jack Mabson.

"All ready," he said. He was beginning to look less strained.

A rosy-cheeked woman came out of the house into the yard. "Well, children," she asked. "How about some of my fruitcake?"

Dr. Emily looked at Mandy and James. "You go ahead," she said. "I'll call you to see the calf." She hurried into the cowshed with Jack.

Mandy and James went with Mrs. Mabson into the big farm kitchen. There was a wood fire burning and two comfortable armchairs drawn up to it. On the scrubbed kitchen table was a huge fruitcake, still warm from the oven. It smelled wonderful. Mrs. Mabson poured a big mug of milk for each of them, but Mandy found her eyes going to the clock again and again. Minutes ticked by. Thirty, forty. She could hardly bear the suspense.

Just when she thought she would burst with the effort of sitting still, there was a sound at the door and Jack Mabson came in. Mandy's heart stopped for a moment. Then she saw that his face was wreathed in smiles. "A fine little heifer," he said. "Just like her mother."

Mandy and James were up out of their chairs in a flash.

"Go ahead," said Jack. "It's a wonderful sight."

They were out of the door and into the cowshed in an instant. "Shh," said Mandy as they went from the sunlight into the warm, sweet-smelling shadows of the shed. Then she saw it — a newborn calf curled under her mother's front legs. Molly was licking her calf, coaxing her into wakefulness.

Dr. Emily stood by them proudly. Her calving gown was rolled up at her feet, and she was pulling down her sleeves. "Isn't she a beauty?" she said. "Just like her mother."

Mandy looked in wonder at the little calf. Her coat was golden where shafts of sunlight found their way into the cowshed. "Oh, Mom," she breathed.

"Do you want to stay for a while?" asked Dr.

Emily. "I think I'll try some of Mrs. Mabson's cake and a cup of tea."

Mandy nodded, her eyes shining.

"We'll be very quiet," said James. "We won't move a muscle."

Dr. Emily laughed. "I doubt if Molly would notice," she said. "She's too busy with her calf."

"What are you going to call her?" asked Mandy just as Jack and his wife came into the cowshed.

Jack laughed. "Well," he said, "I figure that's for you to say. Your mom's brought both heifers into the world. She gave Molly her name, so I think it's only right you should name this little one."

"Oh, thank you," said Mandy. She turned to James. "What shall we call her?"

James grinned. "She's a girl. You choose," he said.

"Goldie," Mandy said as she watched the sun strike another patch of gold on the little calf's flank. "We'll call her Goldie."

What a day! She had found Prince and seen a newborn calf. What a wonderful day!

Six

The next morning Mandy was out of bed and down to the veterinary clinic before breakfast. She wanted to see how the kitten was doing.

Dr. Adam was in the treatment room. "You're early this morning," he said jokingly. "How was the calf?"

Mandy spent a marvelous ten minutes telling him about Goldie as she started cleaning out the small animals' cages. She stopped to help her father as he changed the dressing on Cally's hind leg. He picked up the little tortoiseshell kitten and tucked her firmly into the crook of his arm while Mandy smoothed some ointment on the bad gash in her leg.

"There," she said gently to the kitten. "And don't go playing with sharp farm tools again." Cally mewed and tried to lick the ointment off her back leg, but Dr. Adam wound a fresh bandage deftly around the wound before she could get to it.

"She's very alert this morning," Mandy said. Then to the kitten she said, "Look at Toby. He isn't making a fuss about his leg." Toby the puppy looked up at her and wagged his tail. Mandy put the kitten gently back in her cage and picked him up. He licked her nose.

"So what about Prince? Do they want a visit?" Dr. Adam asked.

Mandy put the puppy back and unlatched the hamsters' cage. She let one of them run up her sleeve. The little creature seemed to be doing well. "No," she said. "Susan might be coming down to the fairgrounds tonight. I thought maybe . . ."

"I could just happen to drop by," said Dr. Adam.

Mandy turned to him. "Oh, Dad, would you? I mean she might not even be there."

"She looks after him all right, doesn't she?" asked Dr. Adam.

Mandy bit her lip. It felt like tattling, but then

Prince was the important thing. "The gardener is supposed to look after him, but he doesn't know anything about horses. He told me so himself."

Dr. Adam came around and stood in front of her as she stroked Tommy's hamster. "You know Prince has always been a healthy pony," he said. "Strong as a horse, you might say."

"Oh, Dad," groaned Mandy. Her father was always saying silly things.

"But seriously," said Dr. Adam, "I don't think you have anything to worry about. I saw Prince only a few weeks ago when Mrs. Jackson decided to sell him. He was absolutely fine then."

"Not coughing?" asked Mandy

Dr. Adam shook his head. "Sound as a bell. But sometimes moving a pony from one home to another can upset it. Believe it or not, Mandy, Prince could just be taking a while to settle in. Odd little ailments aren't unusual in these circumstances. Ponies can be very sensitive creatures."

"You mean he might be homesick?" asked Mandy.

"He might be," said Dr. Adam. "Sometimes animals pine — just like people."

Mandy thought of Susan. Maybe she was taking a while to settle in, too. Maybe she was homesick and that was what was making her so difficult.

"Prince was very glad to see me," said Mandy. *And Susan didn't like that,* she thought.

"See there," said Dr. Adam. "A familiar voice, a person he recognized. It sounds as if he might be pining a little."

Mandy smiled. "That's probably all it is, Dad," she said, "But —"

"But I'll see him just as soon as I get the chance," said Dr. Adam. "Only promise me one thing."

"What?" asked Mandy.

Dr. Adam ruffled her hair. "Don't go getting yourself all worked up about it. It's probably nothing at all."

"Okay," said Mandy. "I promise." She gave the hamster a last cuddle and slid it back into its cage.

"Breakfast," Dr. Emily called from the door. "Just the two of us, Mandy. There's been a call for you, Adam. Metcalf's Farm. It's Shep. He got one of his hind legs caught on some barbed wire, and John Metcalf can't get him free without doing more damage."

Mandy looked up. "Poor Shep," she said. Shep was the Metcalfs' prize sheepdog. They had had him for years.

"He'll be okay," Dr. Emily said. "John is staying with him until Dad gets there, just to make sure he doesn't pull against the wire and hurt himself even more."

Dr. Adam was already on his way out of the door as Mandy and her mother sat down to breakfast. Mandy shook her head. A vet's life was certainly a busy one.

Breakfast was almost over when there was a tap at the door. Grandma came bustling in with a letter in one hand and a bundle of rolled-up posters sticking out of her shoulder bag. Grandma had really taken to writing letters since she'd started the village campaign to save their post office. She waved the letter at them. "She's coming," she said. "She said yes."

Dr. Emily smiled and lifted another cup and saucer down from the china cabinet behind her. "Who's coming where?" she said to Grandma.

Mandy grinned. She watched as Grandma sat herself down and pulled a bundle of handbills and posters out of her bag. She spread them on the table. Dr. Emily made space for the cup and saucer and poured a cup of tea.

"Miranda Jones," Grandma said, taking a sip of tea. "Mmm, that's perfect. Just what I needed." She unrolled one of the posters. Across the top in big letters were the words WELFORD COUNTY FAIR and underneath was a list of all the events. Grandma stabbed a finger at some words at the bottom of the page: PRIZES TO BE PRESENTED BY.

"The Committee left some posters blank till the very last minute," said Grandma, "hoping she would say yes. We just put 'a local celebrity' on the first batch. So all we have to do now is fill in 'Miranda Jones' here along the bottom and we can start putting up the posters and handing out leaflets."

Mandy took a leaflet from the pile. There was a gap at the bottom of those, too. "Do you have to fill in the name on all of these?" she asked. "It'll take you ages."

Grandma's eyes twinkled. "I thought you might give me a hand," she said. "You could give them out at school and put up some posters between here and Welford."

Mandy laughed. "Okay," she said.

Dr. Emily was studying the poster. "And what does Mrs. Ponsonby say about this?" she asked.

Grandma took another sip of tea and said casually, "Oh, she doesn't know yet. I mean there was no point in telling her until we were sure. Besides, nobody had actually asked her to give out the prizes."

"Nobody ever does," said Dr. Emily, "but she does it every year. She must think she's the local celebrity."

"Mmm," said Grandma and had another sip of her tea.

"You do make good tea, Emily. Now tell me, how is your speech going?"

Mandy giggled. Grandma was really good at changing the subject when it suited her. Even Mom gave in.

"It's going really well," said Dr. Emily. "I've nearly finished writing it. Now all I have to do is learn it."

"What's it about, Mom?" said Mandy. Dr. Emily had been asked to give a speech to a conference for vets in York quite soon. Mandy was really proud of her. Imagine all those vets listening to her mom!

"Allergies," Dr. Emily said. "Animals get allergies just like people do, and with all these new pesticides and fertilizers around, farmers have to be very careful."

"What kind of allergies?" Mandy asked.

Dr. Emily shrugged. "All kinds," she said. "Skin rashes, stomach upsets, breathing problems."

"What, like asthma?" said Mandy. Kate had asthma, and when she got an attack she was really breathless. She had been taken to the hospital a few times when it was especially bad. Mandy knew it could be dangerous.

"Like that," said Dr. Emily, "but there's one I'm quite interested in. It's called SAD."

"SAD?" asked Mandy.

Dr. Emily nodded. "It stands for Small Airway Disease. It's like Chronic Obstructive Pulmonary Disease, but SAD is easier to say. People used to have different names for it like broken wind or the heaves."

"Grandpa was talking about the heaves the other day," said Mandy. "Duke has that."

Dr. Emily nodded. "Duke didn't always have it. It can come on at any time, really."

There was a familiar sound outside — gravel spurting and a bicycle bell pinging. James. Mandy stood up.

"Don't forget these," said Grandma, thrusting a pile of handbills and posters at her.

Mandy stuffed them in her backpack. "When is this talk, Mom?" she asked as she tried to get all the leaflets and posters into her bag.

Dr. Emily sighed. "Saturday, unfortunately," she said.

Mandy stopped, all thoughts of posters and allergies banished from her mind. "But you'll miss the Welford County Fair," she said.

Dr. Emily nodded. "It can't be helped," she said.

Mandy looked at her sympathetically. "That's really bad luck, Mom," she said.

"Your dad will be there," Dr. Emily said. "He'll be on duty. It's his turn this year."

"What a pity," said Grandma. "You'll miss Miranda Jones giving out the prizes. She's my favorite. I just love *Parson's Close*."

"Mmm," said Dr. Emily, "*if* Miranda Jones is doing it."

"What do you mean, '*if*'?" asked Grandma, but she didn't sound as confident as usual.

Mandy grinned as she shot out of the door to meet James. Thank goodness she wouldn't be around when Mrs. Ponsonby found out she wasn't the local celebrity after all!

Seven

Mandy got a nice surprise on the way to school. Prince was in the paddock of The Beeches, kicking up his heels and cantering around the field. "Look," she said to James, and they pulled their bikes over to the side of the road.

Mandy leaned over the fence and called the pony's name. At once his ears pricked up, and he came trotting across the short turf toward her. She put her arms around his neck. "Hello, boy," she said, and he whinnied and snuffled at her hair. Mandy giggled. "That tickles," she said to him.

"Someone's coming," James said.

Mandy looked up. Jim, the gardener, was walking

down the paddock toward them. He gave them a wave. "Got to take him back now," he said. "I only let him out while I mucked out his stable. I don't get time to do it very often."

Mandy rubbed Prince's nose. "What a shame," she said. "Do you have to? He seems so happy out here."

"Susan's orders," said Jim "She doesn't want his cold to get worse."

"Oh, well," said Mandy. "I suppose he has to keep warm, but really he seems fine." And he did. There was no sign of a cough. "I'm glad about that anyway," Mandy said to James as they watched Jim lead Prince away. "He really does seem much better."

She said so to Susan when she saw her at school. Susan frowned. "He shouldn't be out at all," she said. "I want him in good condition for the Welford County Fair."

"You're entering, then?" asked Mandy.

Susan sniffed. "I'd better," she said. "After all, my mother is going to be giving out the prizes. She phoned me this morning to tell us. I've decided to enter Prince in the jumps."

"Oh, good," said Mandy. "My grandmother is really pleased."

Susan gave her a puzzled look and opened her

mouth to say something, but Miss Potter called the class to order and started the geography lesson, so it wasn't until break that Susan grabbed Mandy's arm and asked, "What's your grandmother got to do with me entering Prince in the trials?"

"Not the trials. The prize giving," Mandy said. "The Welford Women's Club wrote to your mom asking if she would come and do it since she has connections with Welford now. We can put her name on the posters."

Susan looked as if she didn't know whether to be annoyed or not.

"She's famous, isn't she?" asked Mandy.

"Of course she's famous," Susan said.

"Well, then," said Mandy, "it'll be good for the fair."

Susan looked undecided. "And I'm glad you're entering Prince," Mandy went on. "They give marks for grooming, you know. I could help you with that if you want."

For a moment she thought Susan was going to say "Don't bother" or "It's none of your business." Then she saw a change come over her face. Susan's eyes lit up. "If I won, then Mom would be giving the prize to me, wouldn't she?"

Mandy nodded. "I suppose so."

Susan's eyes grew dreamy. "I *will* enter, then,"

she said. "And I'll win." And with that she marched off to her next class.

Mandy didn't see much of her for the rest of the day, but she was so busy writing in MIRANDA JONES in big letters and passing out handfuls of leaflets and posters to people that she hardly noticed.

"Why is it Miranda *Jones*?" Melanie asked. "Susan's name is Collins."

"Jones is her stage name," said Mandy.

Melanie sniffed. "Not very fancy, is it? It should be something romantic — like Honeychurch or Smythe-Bassington-Jones."

Mandy shook her head. She was glad it wasn't Miranda Smythe-Bassington-Jones. It would take too long to write.

She caught up with James at lunchtime. "I've done all mine," he said. "Now it's just the ones we have to hang up on the way home from school."

"Great," said Mandy. "See you at three-thirty. I still have a few more to give out."

By the time three-thirty came, all the kids from the outlying districts had their posters to put up in the villages and farms. It took Mandy and James three times longer than usual to get from Walton to Welford. They had put up posters at the end of every farm road.

Prince wasn't in the paddock when they passed The Beeches. But she hoped she would see him tonight. It was a pity he had to be inside on such a nice day. Maybe he missed that. Jane had always put him out to crop grass in good weather.

"There," said Mandy as they posted the last one at the Fox and Goose. "Nobody could miss them. It should be a great turnout for the fair."

Mr. Hardy, the owner of the Fox and Goose, came out to admire it. "Yes," he said. "That looks great. And if you give me some posters I'll leave them where people can pick them up."

"Thanks, Mr. Hardy," Mandy said, handing him a stack of posters.

Mr. Hardy looked at their red faces. "It's thirsty work hanging signs," he said. "You sit down and I'll get you a glass of lemonade."

They got off their bikes and settled themselves on the bench outside the pub. In a moment two hands appeared out of the open window above James's shoulder. The hands were holding two brimming glasses of lemonade and two bags of potato chips.

Mandy smiled. "Thanks, Mr. Hardy."

"We can certainly use these," said James, taking the glasses.

Mr. Hardy leaned over the window ledge and

winked. "As I said, thirsty work," he said to them. "Enjoy!"

They were still sitting on the bench polishing off the last of the lemonade when Mrs. Ponsonby came by on her way to the village hall.

Mrs. Ponsonby was a large woman with a blue hair rinse and pink eyeglasses. She came down the street like a ship in full sail. She was carrying a large bundle of decorations under one arm and a very fat Pekingese under the other. She looked at them as she passed and said disapprovingly. "Whatever would your grandmother say, Mandy Hope?" she said. "Sitting outside a tavern in broad daylight."

"It would be worse sitting outside a tavern in the dark," James muttered. But Mrs. Ponsonby didn't hear, for at that moment the Peke gave a shrill yap and tried to make a dive for Mandy's chips.

"Now, now, Pandora my precious," Mrs. Ponsonby said. Then she noticed the poster stuck up on the door of the Fox and Goose. "What's this?" she asked. It was one of James's posters. He had written Susan's mom's name in great big red letters with a felt-tipped pen. Mrs. Ponsonby opened her mouth twice, but she was so mad she couldn't speak. Then she got her voice back. "Miranda

WELFORD
✿ SHOW ✿
1:00pm   Sat
Raffle TOMBOLA
    Pet Corner
HORSE SHOW
         CAKES
  Refreshments
PRIZES TO BE
PRESENTED BY
MIRANDA
JONES
...ssion - 50p

Jones," she said. "*Miranda Jones*. The others said a local celebrity. Who is Miranda Jones?"

"She's on TV," Mandy said. "In *Parson's Close*. She's the pastor's wife. She's famous. Her husband has bought that big new house on the Walton road. That's what makes her 'local.'"

Mandy stopped as Mrs. Ponsonby looked at her. Pandora yelped. Mrs. Ponsonby must have tightened her grip.

"And whose idea was this?" she said. "No, don't tell me. I can guess." She loosened her grip on Pandora and shook the bundle of decorations at them. "We'll see about this," she said. "We'll just see about this." And she turned on her heel and marched off majestically down the hill to the village hall.

"I pity your poor grandmother," said James.

Mandy smiled. "Somehow I don't think Grandma will be too bothered. The WWC committee decided to ask Susan's mom. They're all fed up with Mrs. Ponsonby." She sighed. "It's Pandora I feel sorry for."

"Why does she carry her everywhere?" said James. "Why doesn't she let her walk?"

Mandy sighed. "Poor Pandora is too fat to walk very far," Mandy said. "Mrs. Ponsonby overfeeds her. She even gives her sweets. It's so bad for her teeth and it could make Pandora sick."

"Oh, well," said James. "If I don't go I won't be fed at all." He got up. "See you tonight," he said. "Seven o'clock at the field."

"Mmm," said Mandy, getting up reluctantly. Sitting in the sun drinking lemonade really was nice. Then she remembered Cally and Toby and Tommy's hamsters and wondered if there were any new animals at Animal Ark today. She was up and onto her bike in an instant. "See you later," she called as she whizzed down the road toward home.

There was a new patient at Animal Ark, a guinea pig.

"Go in and see it," said Simon. "Your dad won't mind. He has Johnny Foster and three of his friends in there already." Johnny Foster was nine and lived near James.

Mandy slipped into the treatment room and caught her dad's eye. "What's wrong with him?" she said as she approached the treatment table. Four boys stood around the table looking at the guinea pig.

"He's losing weight," said Dr. Adam as he turned to Johnny. "What do you feed him?"

Johnny drew himself up. "All the best things," he said. "Food from the pet shop in Walton and carrots and lettuce and apples. But he doesn't want to eat anything. He's so thin. I'm scared he's going to die."

Dr. Adam laid a hand on Johnny's shoulder. "Now look, Johnny," he said. "Your guinea pig isn't going to die. I promise you that, but do you see these teeth?" Dr. Adam pointed at the two sharp incisor teeth. Johnny nodded. "Guinea pigs' teeth aren't like ours," Dr. Adam said. "They grow all the time. When they get too long it makes it difficult for them to eat. They need something to wear their teeth down. A block of wood will do, just so long as he can rasp his teeth against it and get a good chew."

"Will he have to go to the dentist and get them out?" asked Johnny.

Dr. Adam laughed. "No," he said. "All I have to do is clip them. He won't feel it. His teeth aren't like ours. It's just like cutting your fingernails."

Johnny didn't look convinced.

"Look," said Dr. Adam. "You watch me, and if you think I'm hurting him then I'll stop right away."

He gave the guinea pig to Mandy. "Hold him," he said. He selected a pair of small stainless steel clippers from the sterilizing unit. A couple of quick snips and it was done. Mandy gave the guinea pig a tickle under the chin. He really was very thin. Then she handed him to Johnny.

At once Johnny reached into his pocket and brought out a rather dusty-looking piece of carrot. The guinea-pig eyed it for a moment and then seized on it. It was gone in seconds. Johnny's face lit up.

"He's hungry again," he said. "He's eating!"

And he and his three friends trooped out of the treatment room.

"Feeding animals properly is really important, isn't it, Dad?" Mandy said. She was thinking of Mrs. Ponsonby's dog.

"Feeding people is pretty important, too," said Dr. Adam. "That was my last patient. Let's get washed up. Your mom's been out all day doing tuberculin injections and she'll be exhausted, so we're going to give her a break. You and I are going to make dinner."

Mandy and her dad got busy in the kitchen, and by the time Mom came in dinner was nearly ready.

Dr. Emily was delighted. "This is wonderful," she said as she sat down at the table.

They chatted over dinner. Dr. Emily had managed to call in at Baildon. "Goldie sends her love," she said. "And there's something in my coat pocket for you, Mandy."

Mandy raced out to the hall and burrowed in her mother's pockets. She felt a thin piece of card, which she drew out, and there she was. Goldie, the calf, standing sturdy and strong beside her mother.

"Look, Dad," she said as he came out to the hall

after her. "It's Goldie, the new calf. Mr. Mabson must have taken a picture of her."

Dr. Adam looked at the picture and smiled. "That's one that's going to get center stage on your wall," he said. Then he lowered his voice. "Look, Mandy," he said. "Your mom's really tired, so I think she should get straight to bed and have a good night's rest. So that means I have to be here on call."

Mandy nodded. "So you won't be able to come down to the field to see Prince?" she asked. She smiled. "It's all right, Dad. I saw him this morning on my way to school and he was his old self again."

Dr. Adam smiled. "In any case I'll see him at the fair," he said. "I'm on duty, remember?"

Mandy agreed. But there would be no need. Prince was better now.

Eight

James was already there when Mandy got down to Redpath's field just before seven o'clock. He was sitting on the churchyard wall waiting for her. "It's looking good," he said.

Mandy looked around. It certainly was looking good. There were several tents up already, flags were fluttering from trestle tables set up around the edges of the field, and everywhere there were groups of people hammering stalls together, roping off areas of the field, setting up raffle stands, and piling bales of hay into tiers for the horse jumping. Over on the far side Mandy could see her grandfather and Walter Pickard. She waved to them, and Grandpa called her over.

"Ready for some hard work?" he said as they reached them.

Mandy and James nodded, and Grandpa handed them each a bucket of water and a brush. "Right," he said. "The first thing to do is get these jumps washed down. They have to be in tiptop condition for Saturday."

"Even the one made out of hay bales?" James joked.

Grandpa grinned. "No, I suppose you can leave that one," he said.

Mandy and James started to work. The jumps were spaced around the area that had been roped off for the pony trials. They scrubbed at them with the long-handled brushes. The red-and-white poles stretched across their supports became brighter. Even the painted bricks of the "wall" jumps shone brick red. It was hard work, but they were enjoying being part of the team working to make the fair a success.

They had almost finished when Mandy heard a car pull up. She turned to see a dark green horse trailer towed by a blue sports car pull onto the field. Susan. That was her dad's car.

Mandy put down her brush. "James," she said, "Susan's here with Prince."

James looked up from a five-bar gate he was scrubbing. "Just so long as she doesn't get these jumps dirty," he said. "I'm exhausted."

Mr. Collins was unlocking the horse trailer and letting down the ramp. Mandy stood, brush in hand, and watched as Prince stepped delicately down the ramp and onto the grass. She saw his head go up sniffing the air, and then he coughed. "He's coughing again," she said to James. "He was fine this morning. I wish Dad had been able to come down after all."

James looked at her. "You know what your dad said. Prince has always been a healthy pony."

Mandy pursed her lips. "He doesn't sound too healthy now."

Susan took Prince's halter and led him to the edge of the ring, tethering him to a post. Then she walked off toward where Grandpa and Walter were talking to some other helpers.

"Come on," said Mandy. "Let's go and see him."

Dropping her brush, she sprinted across to where Prince was tethered. As she approached he coughed again but not as deeply as he had before. She felt his flank. It was warm and dry. As she ran her hand gently down the pony's side, some hay dust rose from his coat in a little cloud.

"He needs a good brushing," said James, but Mandy wasn't listening. She had her ear pressed close to Prince's flank. She could hear the breath deep in his chest. Was it her imagination or did it sound odd, not steady the way it usually was? She turned a troubled face to James.

"Is there something wrong with him?" said James.

Mandy just shook her head in puzzlement and continued stroking Prince's flank. As she did so she felt his breath steady. She rubbed his nose, and his ears twitched toward her. "How are you, boy?" she said.

Prince nuzzled her shoulder and whinnied. "That's odd," said Mandy. "He seems all right now. Yet I'm sure his breathing was funny before."

"Here comes Susan," said James.

Susan was striding across the field toward them. She was carrying a saddle. "I'm going to try the jumps now," she said.

"I'll help you saddle up," said Mandy.

For a moment she thought Susan was going to refuse her help. But Susan just said, "If you like," and slung the saddle over Prince's back.

As they adjusted the girth and let down the stirrups Mandy said carefully, "He was coughing again."

"I know," said Susan. She looked puzzled. Mandy tried to hide her surprise. Maybe she wasn't going to yell at her for interfering. "But Jim let him out for a while today — you saw him. Maybe he got chilled." She looked at the pony. "But he's all right now, isn't he?"

Mandy had to agree. There seemed to be nothing wrong with the pony. "See how he goes over the jumps," she said. "If you don't think he's fit you don't have to do it. You don't have to enter him in the trials at all."

Susan looked at her in disbelief. "Not enter him?" she said. "Who said anything about not entering him? Of course I'm going to enter him. I have to. I'm going to make Mom so proud of me she'll — " She stopped.

"What?" said Mandy, but just then Grandpa and Walter arrived. What was it Susan had been going to say?

"Why don't you walk him around the jumps first," Grandpa was saying to Susan. "Just to see if we have the spacing about right. Then we can put him to the fences."

Mandy watched as Susan led Prince away. First she showed him each jump, letting him take his time investigating it, getting to know it. Then she got up on him and walked him around the course, just skirting the fences, pacing them, getting the feel of the layout. And only then did she urge him into a trot and then a canter around the outskirts of the field before bringing him up to the jumps at the gallop.

The first two jumps went smoothly. Prince sailed over them, his tail arching gracefully, his hooves clearing the bars by inches. At the third he was wrongfooted, and Susan turned him easily aside and slowed him to a trot before trying it again. Once again he was wrongfooted, half a pace out on the approach. Susan slowed him to a walk this time.

"I think this one is a little off," she called to Grandpa. "The angle coming into the fence doesn't seem right."

Grandpa and Walter went into a huddle, then moved the jump back a little and to the side so that the angle was wider. "Try that," Grandpa called back to her.

Susan took a long, slow approach to the fence, giving Prince plenty of time to refuse, not forcing him. He flew over it like a dream.

The only other fence that gave Prince any trouble was the fifth jump, the one made of hay bales. He simply refused it. Susan was clearly puzzled. She tried him three times in all. The third time Prince took the jump but he wasn't happy. His head came up straining at the bit as he came over.

After that Prince had no trouble. Susan leaned over and patted him as they cleared the last jump. Mandy saw her bend to whisper in his ear. Prince seemed absolutely fine, hardly out of breath, but then Susan had taken the jumps easily, giving him time where he needed it, not pushing him on from jump to jump

"She's good, isn't she?" said James.

Mandy nodded. She was surprised. Susan boasted so much about everything, it was hard to believe she really was good at show jumping. "She's better than Barry Prescott," Mandy said. Barry sometimes forced Star.

"Look," said Mandy. Susan had taken Prince right around the outside of the jumps. She was going to go for a full circuit. Mandy saw her turn Prince at the far end of the field, gather the reins firmly in her hands, and point him toward the first jump.

Mandy held her breath. Susan and the little pony seemed to melt into each other. Looking at her as she cleared first one fence, then the next, Mandy couldn't imagine Susan ever falling off — or Prince ever failing to clear a jump.

Then as they thundered up the field toward Mandy and James, Mandy saw Prince's head go up. He was trying to turn away from the hay bales. Horse and rider faced them head on. Mandy saw Susan's mouth set, saw her gather the reins more tightly, touch her heels to the pony's flanks — and he was over. But his eyes were rolling.

Susan and Prince were around the top of the field, heading for the last three jumps. Prince cleared them, but Mandy was running toward the finish with James behind her.

"What's wrong?" he yelled as he pelted after her.

"Didn't you see his eyes?" Mandy shouted back. "He didn't want to try that jump. He isn't happy."

Susan was drawing Prince to a walk as they arrived. She slowed him to a halt. "Pretty good," she said, "but he should be able to do even better."

Mandy laid a hand on Prince's flank. She felt his chest plunge and ripple.

"It was too much for him," she panted. "Look at him. He's so out of breath."

Susan looked down at her. Her smile had disappeared. "Oh, come on," she said. "He's just jumped a clear round. You would be out of breath if you had done that. You're out of breath as it is and you've only run half the length of the course."

Mandy bit her lip. It sounded so reasonable, but she had watched Jane jump Prince many times. She had never seen Prince as out of breath as this.

"She's got a point," said James.

Mandy turned to him. "Whose side are you on?" she asked.

James looked surprised. "Nobody's," he said. "It isn't about taking sides, is it?"

Susan smirked down at Mandy. "It is as far as Mandy's concerned." She patted Prince's neck. "Come on, Prince," she said. "At least I think you did well even though some people think you aren't up to it."

"It isn't that," said Mandy. Then she stopped. After all, it was what she was saying — that Prince wasn't up to it.

Grandpa and Walter came up to them.

"That was fine," said Walter, "and thanks for your help, Susan."

Susan smiled down at him. "He's a good jumper, isn't he?" she said.

Walter smiled. "He is," he said.

"He's a great jumper," said Grandpa, but Mandy saw him looking at the pony. Prince was still breathing heavily, and Grandpa was looking at his flanks, puzzled.

"Yes," said Walter. "The only better jumper around here is that bay gelding of Barry Prescott's. He usually walks off with the prize in the jumping. He's very fast."

Susan slid down off Prince and looked at them. "Not this year he won't," she said. "You'll see. Prince can jump faster than that. Just you wait till the fair. Now that I know he can clear the jumps, all he needs is a bit more speed."

"Susan," said Mandy.

Susan had begun to walk Prince toward the horse trailer. She turned to Mandy. "What is it now?" she said.

Mandy took a deep breath. "You won't push Prince too hard at the fair, will you?" she said.

"Because you don't think he's up to it?" said Susan scornfully. "You just can't bear to see me win. But we will win, Mandy Hope. You'll see. All he had was a little cold, and of course he's out of breath jumping. A day in a warm, dry stable and he'll be fit for anything. He can go faster than that. I know he can. Barry Prescott won't win this year. I will — whatever happens." And, her face grim with determination, she unsaddled Prince and led him into the horse trailer.

Mandy looked as Susan tethered the pony. There was a hay net secured at the far end of the trailer and Mandy plucked a handful and began rubbing Prince down. Then she dropped the hay to the floor of the trailer. Prince stamped and coughed. Susan turned to Mandy.

"It's just a cold," she said and, walking down the ramp, began to secure the back door of the trailer.

As Mandy turned away she saw Susan's father come out of the tent at the far end of the field and begin to walk toward the car. She wandered over to where she had left Grandpa. He was still standing there. He looked thoughtful.

"What's the matter, Grandpa?" she asked.

Grandpa scratched his head. "I'm not sure," he said. "It was when I was standing there looking at Prince. It reminded me of something, but I can't for the life of me remember what it is." He shook his head. "Old age, Mandy," he said. "I must be getting on in years."

Mandy smiled, but she wasn't really paying attention. All she could think of were Susan's last words. She would win, whatever happened. Mandy would speak to her father again. He was on duty at the fair. He *had* to look at Prince before the jumping. She hated to think what would happen if Susan rode Prince flat out. She remembered the panic and fear in Prince's eyes. A cold chill seemed to settle on her heart.

Nine

It was Saturday morning, the day of the Welford County Fair. Mandy was looking forward to seeing Prince. He hadn't been out in the paddock at all yesterday when they passed to and from school, and Mandy hadn't dared to ask Susan how he was in case she snapped her head off. In any case, Susan was keeping out of her way.

Mandy jumped out of bed and dived for the bathroom. A quick shower, a clean pair of jeans, a fresh shirt, and she was off, taking the stairs two at a time.

Dr. Emily was checking her papers for the conference, and Dr. Adam was checking on the animals in the veterinary office. "Are you taking Toby to the fair?" he asked Mandy as he came out of the treatment room.

"What about his leg, Dad?" she asked.

Dr. Adam smiled. "Come and see," he said.

Mandy followed him into the unit. There was Toby in his cage — with no cast on his leg. "He's better," she said.

Dr. Adam nodded. "Good as new," he said. "The leg will need a lot of exercise, but he's young, so it won't be long before he's running around as good as new."

"Then he doesn't need to stay in here any longer," Mandy said.

Dr. Adam laughed. "Bring him through," he said.

Mandy set Toby down on the floor. He was still a little unbalanced, but that was only because he wasn't used to having four fully working legs yet. It wouldn't be long before he was racing around.

Dr. Adam said he would check Prince out just as soon as he arrived at the fair. Mandy felt as if a weight had been lifted off her. She knew her father wouldn't let Prince overstrain himself.

"What are his symptoms?" Dr. Emily asked.

"He gets really out of breath when Susan jumps him," said Mandy.

"Jumping is hard work," said Dr. Emily.

Mandy shook her head. "I know," she said slowly, "but he coughs sometimes when he's just standing still. It doesn't seem to make any sense."

Dr. Emily gathered up the rest of her papers and looked at her watch. "I'd better go," she said, "or I'll be late." Then she hesitated, looking at the papers in her hand. "You know," she said, "it could be an allergy of some sort."

"Would that be serious?" asked Mandy.

Dr. Emily frowned. "It might be. It depends what kind of allergy you're talking about. It's a complicated business."

Dr. Adam smiled. "Your head is full of allergies this morning," he said. "But I'll check it out."

"I suppose you're right," said Dr. Emily.

Mandy and her father went to the door to wave good-bye to Mom.

"Tommy Pickard is coming to pick up his hamsters this morning," Dr. Adam said.

Mandy grinned. "He wants to put them in the Family Pets section at the fair." She thought for a moment "Who's judging it?"

Dr. Adam coughed. "I am," he said.

Mandy shook her head. "You were keeping that a secret," she said. "Poor Dad. What a job!"

"And I'll know most of the animals as well as the owners," Dr. Adam said. "I wish they had asked somebody else." He sighed. "Maybe I'll just close my eyes, turn around three times and point. Anyway, let's get a move on."

They didn't have any time to spare. By nine-thirty when James arrived, they had done all the medications and finished the dressings.

James had Blackie with him. Dr. Adam gave the black Labrador a pat, and Blackie looked up at him adoringly. Blackie was a typical Labrador, friends with the whole world.

"How are the tricks coming along, James?" asked Dr. Adam.

James grinned. "Watch," he said. He took a big red bandanna from his pocket, held it under Blackie's nose, and disappeared into the hall with it. Then he came back and said to Blackie, "Find!"

Blackie looked up at him, waved his tail, barked, and licked his hand.

"Find!" said James again.

Blackie woofed happily, and his tail wagged even faster.

Dr. Adam laughed. "You have a long way to go there, James," he said.

James shook his head. "He just doesn't seem to get the message."

"Unless it's feathers," Mandy said, and she and James laughed.

"I've got to run," Dr. Adam said. He turned to Mandy. "Can you stay here until Tommy comes to get the hamsters?"

Mandy nodded. "No problem. You go on ahead."

"Okay," said Dr. Adam, picking up his bag and making for the door.

Mandy was smiling. "Dad, wouldn't it be better to change out of your slippers?"

Dr. Adam looked down. "Thanks, Mandy. I'd look like a real idiot showing up in these, wouldn't I?" He found his shoes, shoved his feet into them, and picked up the slippers.

Mandy took them from him. "Go," she said, almost shoving him out of the door. "You'll be late."

"I'm going," he said. He grabbed his bag and went out through the office door.

Mandy put the slippers neatly in a corner, and she and James followed to wave good-bye.

Mandy ran after the car. "Don't forget to have a look at Prince," she shouted.

Dr. Adam waved. "I'll remember," he said. "Don't worry."

"See you later," called Mandy. She looked around her. "Where's Toby?"

"Where's Blackie?" said James.

They soon tracked them down — in the living room. In his hurry, Dr. Adam had left the door between the office and the house open. Mandy looked at what had once been one of her dad's best slippers. It was a mangled mess. Toby looked guilty and dropped the slipper.

Mandy picked up the puppy and looked into his big brown eyes. "Oh, you naughty thing," she said, cuddling it. The puppy licked her nose and wagged his stumpy tail.

James picked up the slipper. "Tell me your dad didn't really like these slippers," he said.

Mandy made a face. "They were his favorites," she said. "I don't know what he'll say."

"Can I have my hamsters now?" said a little voice from the doorway. It was Tommy Pickard. "The door was open, so I just came in," he said.

"Wait here," said Mandy. "I'll get them."

She went through to the office and collected the hamster cage. As she came back she carefully shut the door between the office and the house. "Here," she said, giving the cage to Tommy.

Just then James gave a yell. "He's done it! He's found the bandanna! Good boy, Blackie. Good boy." He put his arms around Blackie's neck.

"Oops," Tommy said. "I didn't mean to."

Mandy looked around. The cage door was wide-open. The three hamsters shot out.

"Tommy!" said Mandy, then she stopped as she saw what was happening.

One hamster was halfway up the curtains, another had gone under the sofa, and the third was burrowing under the fireside rug. Toby looked as if he couldn't decide which one to chase first. Blackie just sat there for a moment, then he dropped the red bandanna and started to pull at the fireside rug.

"Get Toby!" Mandy yelled to James.

James made a dive for the puppy, missed, and fell flat on his face — across the hearth rug. A very startled hamster shot out from underneath and halfway up the leg of Mandy's jeans. She grabbed the hamster and shoved it into Tommy's hands.

"Put it back in the cage," she said to him, "and shut the door."

The little boy's eyes were wide. "Okay," he said.

"Got you," said James as he finally grabbed hold of Toby. His face was red, his hair was standing on end, and his glasses were knocked sideways — but he had the puppy.

Mandy managed to coax the second hamster out from under the sofa. She went and put that one in the cage.

Tommy was sitting there watching the cage — as if the hamsters might break out again. "Don't move," Mandy said to him. She took Toby from James and gave him to Tommy. "Hold him," she said.

James was standing on a chair trying to reach the last hamster. The one that had shot up the curtains. But the hamster just sat there staring at him until he got too near, then it scampered along to the other end of the curtain rod.

Blackie was following the hamster's movements with his eyes. Mandy couldn't help it. She started to laugh.

"What's so funny?" asked James.

Mandy wiped away tears of laughter. "You," she said. "Every time you get anywhere near it, it just runs away. And then you have to move the chair. And then it runs to the other end of the curtain rod."

"It isn't funny," said James. But he started to laugh as well.

"Come on," said Mandy at last. "Let's try a two-pronged attack."

They got two chairs set up in front of the curtains and at last managed to trap the hamster between them. Mandy made a final lunge and got it. "There," she said, putting it with the others. "And don't open that cage again," she said to Tommy.

Mandy and James watched the little boy set off down the path. Walter Pickard was waiting at the end of the lane. He waved to them as Tommy ran toward him.

"They must be going to the fair," said James.

"And at least *we* can get to the fair now," said Mandy.

But just then the phone rang. Mandy picked it up and spoke for a few moments, then she put the receiver down and turned a worried face to James.

"What is it?" he asked.

"That was Dad," she said. "He's had an urgent call to one of the farms up on the hill."

James was puzzled. "It isn't anything terrible, is it?"

Mandy shook her head. "No," she said. "It isn't that I'm worried about, it's Prince."

"Prince?" asked James.

"Dad was going to look at him, check him over. I knew Dad wouldn't let him jump if he wasn't fit. But Prince and Susan haven't arrived yet, and Dad had to go. So now there won't be anybody to check Prince out." Mandy's heart was beating double-time.

"You're worried, aren't you?" asked James.

Mandy nodded. "I am *now*," she said. "I was depending on Dad being able to see him before the competition." She bit her lip. "This morning Mom said it might be an allergy, and allergies can be dangerous. I just know Susan is going to ride Prince hard. She says she's going to win, whatever happens."

Mandy looked at James. "We have to find out what's wrong with Prince, James. We have to do something!"

Ten

They pedaled as fast as they could. Mandy had put Toby into her bicycle basket. The puppy seemed to enjoy the ride. Blackie ran along at James's side. Soon the village church was in sight — and Farmer Redpath's field behind.

They swerved through the church gate and left their bikes propped against the porch. Mandy tucked Toby under her arm, and they ran around to the low wall at the back of the church and hopped over. It was quicker than going through the gate. At once they were in the middle of the tents and stands.

In the distance Mandy caught a glimpse of Duke

the workhorse all decked out in brasses and ribbons. People called out to her and James, but they didn't stop. She wanted to get to the jumping ring as quickly as possible. She didn't even stop when Jean waved to them from behind the cake and candy stand. Mandy just waved back and kept on running, nearly knocking over the cake display at the cake competition stand.

Mrs. Ponsonby came out from the far end of the cake display stand scolding. She was wearing an enormous pink hat with feathers in it. Pandora, as usual, was under her arm.

"Sorry, Mrs. Ponsonby," Mandy muttered.

"Sorry isn't good enough," said Mrs. Ponsonby. "You should be more careful, young lady," and she stood right in front of Mandy beside the biggest chocolate cake on the stand.

"Sorry," said Mandy again. Toby tried to squirm out of her grasp to make friends with Pandora. Pandora yipped a greeting to Toby. Mrs. Ponsonby gave the puppy a sideways look and shifted Pandora to her other arm. Pandora suddenly became very quiet. Mandy stole a look at her and started to say, "Mrs. Pon —"

But Mrs. Ponsonby was in full swing. Mandy and James got a complete lecture on the manners of the younger generation, society today, and the dangers

of running when you should walk. Finally Mandy could bear it no longer. "Mrs. Ponsonby," she said loudly. "Pandora is eating that chocolate cake."

Mrs. Ponsonby turned in horror. Pandora, still in her arms, was making her way steadily through the cake. "My cake!" screeched Mrs. Ponsonby. "My beautiful cake!" She turned to Mandy. "This is your fault," she said.

Mandy could control her temper no longer. "It isn't my fault," she snapped. "If you didn't give that poor dog sweets all the time she would know better. You have to train dogs. It's for their own good. Poor Pandora can hardly walk, she's so fat. It's not my fault, Mrs. Ponsonby. It's yours!"

Mrs. Ponsonby was so angry she couldn't speak. Even the feathers on her hat trembled in rage. Blackie barked and looked longingly at them. James grabbed his collar with one hand and Mandy's arm with the other. "Come on," he whispered in Mandy's ear. "Let's get out of here, quick."

They left Mrs. Ponsonby still staring after them, speechless.

Then they were at the jumping ring. Mandy looked around. No sign of Susan. Then she caught sight of the blue sports car with the horse trailer in tow. A pretty, fair-haired woman in a flower-patterned dress got out of the car. Mandy recognized her from television. It was Susan's mom.

A few people turned and spotted her. All at once she was surrounded by people with pieces of paper. She began signing autographs.

Susan got out of the back of the car and caught Mandy's eye. "Look," she seemed to say. "Look what a famous mother I have."

Susan looked terrific. Her hair was tucked up under the riding hat, and her boots were polished to a high shine. She went around to the back of the horse trailer and began to undo the ramp.

Mandy's eyes fastened on Prince as he stepped daintily down the ramp. She was a bit far away to tell but she thought he looked winded. But how could he be winded? He had only just arrived.

"What are you going to do?" asked James.

"Try talking to Susan," said Mandy, "but I don't think she'll listen."

They made their way over to the horse trailer. Mandy looked at Prince. His sides were heaving and he was coughing. She took a deep breath. "I don't think you should jump Prince," she said.

Susan's head came up. "What?" she said.

Mandy bit her lip. "I don't think he's well enough. Look at him. He's out of breath."

Susan's eyes hardened. "You just don't want me to win," she said.

"That isn't true," Mandy protested. But Susan wasn't listening.

"Just wait," Susan said. "You'll see what Prince can do." She looked at Mandy. "I've told you it's just a cold. I kept him warm and dry in his stable all day yesterday. He'll be fine. He just needs a bit of exercise. And if you think I'm going to give up without even trying to win you're mistaken." Susan's face suddenly lit up. "Don't you realize?" she said. "If I win Mom is going to be so proud. She might even come and live with us here."

It took a moment for it to sink in. So that was why Susan was so determined to win. It wasn't just the winning after all. Mandy's mind was in a whirl.

Susan looked at her and her face softened. "Look," she said almost kindly, "I have to go and see Mom. You take care of Prince for me. We aren't on until the third group."

Mandy watched her run off across the field. She put Toby down on the grass, turned to Prince, and laid her head against his neck. It felt damp, but his breathing had quieted a little.

"How is he?" asked James.

Mandy turned to him. "I don't know," she said. "I wish Dad were here."

James's mouth set. "I'll go and see if he's back yet," he said, running off.

Mandy watched him go. She didn't think her father would be back yet. And she knew now that there was no way Susan would give up a chance of winning — she wouldn't let herself believe there was anything wrong with Prince. She wanted so much to win to impress her mother.

But it wasn't "just a cold." Susan had been fooling herself. Prince was really ill, and if Susan wasn't going to do anything about it, then Mandy would have to.

Just then a race judge passed by. Mandy stopped him. "I don't think this pony is fit to jump," she said.

He looked at her. "Is he your pony?"

Mandy shook her head. "No, but I think he's sick."

The judge ran a hand over the pony's legs and flanks. "I can't see anything wrong with him. Why don't you take him over to the vet?"

For a moment Mandy's spirits rose. "Is he back?"

James appeared at her elbow. "No luck," he said. "He still isn't here."

Mandy looked at the race judge. The man spread his hands. "There's nothing I can do," he said. "The pony doesn't belong to you, and I'm not a vet." He gave Prince another look. "Anyway, he looks all right to me," he said.

Mandy watched him walk away. She was desperate. She tried to think, but there was so little time. Already a loudspeaker was announcing the pony trials, asking the first group of riders and mounts to assemble. She could see Barry Prescott on his bay gelding, trotting him, warming him up. And Susan was going to try and beat a strong horse like that.

Mandy began to walk Prince over the grass toward the jumping ring. The air blew fresh, and a cool little breeze sprang up. She laid her hand on Prince's flank. His breathing was easier now — hardly noticeable, and he had stopped coughing.

"How's he doing?" asked a voice behind her.

It was Grandpa. He gave Prince a pat. "We miss him, your grandmother and I," he said. "We used to like stopping by to see him in that little lean-to." He scratched his head. "That reminds me," he said. "I must go and make sure that Duke is far away from those hay bales. I don't want him coming down with the heaves. Not that they call it that these days. Got some fancy name for it now. But it doesn't matter what they call it — it could still be dangerous for old Duke."

"Be dangerous for him?" asked Mandy.

Grandpa looked at her. "That time when Duke

got locked in the hay barn. He collapsed — nearly died. Luckily Dan got him out in time. It would have broken Dan's heart if Duke had died." And he strode off across the field.

Mandy watched him for a moment, her mind beginning to work overtime, putting things together. She looked over to where the horse trailer stood empty. Wisps of hay blew about inside it. She turned and looked at the jumping ring, at the jump Prince had refused, the hay bales. She thought of Prince's stable and how warm and dry it was. Dusty dry; dust from the straw on the floor and the hay net. He had been in there all day yesterday.

"What is it?" asked James.

Mandy turned a worried face to him. "They do have a fancy name for it now," she said. "It's called SAD, only I can't remember what that stands for. Mom was talking about it the other day." She clutched James's arm. "James, I'm nearly sure that's what's wrong with Prince. His stable is dusty with hay, not like his old stable. He wheezes when he's been shut up in the horse trailer and he refused the hay bales jump. I think Mom was right. I think he *is* allergic — to hay."

The loudspeaker burst into life again, and the first rider started off around the course. Mandy watched. One fence cleared, the next down, two more cleared, then the hay bales. As the pony's hooves touched the top of the jump, wisps of hay flew up. By the time it was Prince's turn there would be hay blowing about everywhere.

She looked across the field. Susan was standing in a group with Mrs. Ponsonby, Grandma, and Pastor Walters — and her mother. They were having their photos taken.

Maybe Mandy was wrong. Just because the workhorse had an allergy didn't mean Prince had it. Then the last piece of the jigsaw fitted into place. Grandpa had been looking at Prince when he remembered Duke. Prince had reminded him of Duke. Why? The answer came to her loud and clear: They both hated hay.

She looked at Prince. He was breathing easily. He looked as fit as could be. But what if he jumped? Mandy couldn't bear to think about what might happen. She thought of the panic and fear in Prince's eyes as he cleared the hay bale jump. How much worse would that be today? Duke had nearly died from the heaves. Mandy couldn't let that happen to Prince.

She turned to James, her mind made up. "Will you help me?" she asked.

James looked puzzled. "Help you to do what?" he

asked. "You heard the judge. There's nothing we can do."

Mandy's mouth set in a grim line. "Oh, yes, there is," she said.

James looked even more puzzled. "What?"

Mandy's head came up. "We can steal Prince," she said. "Steal him and hide him until the jumping is over or until Dad gets here."

The loudspeaker announced that the second group of ponies was to assemble. "Steal him?" James said in a whisper.

Mandy nodded. "Well? What about it? Are you with me?"

Eleven

James's face was a picture of concern.

"Steal Prince?" he asked again.

Mandy nodded. "To protect him. It's the only way."

"We'll get into big trouble," said James.

"Prince could get into worse trouble," said Mandy. "What if he collapsed on the course? What if he died? Grandpa says Duke nearly did. And Susan is determined to make Prince jump."

James took a deep breath. "Okay, I'm with you," he said. "What do we do?"

Mandy heaved a sigh of relief. She laid her hand

gently on Prince's neck. "The first thing to do is decide where we're going to take him," she said.

"But how are we going to get him away without somebody noticing?" James asked.

Mandy bit her lip in concentration. "You'll have to distract everybody's attention," she said. "Then I can slip Prince out of the show ring when everyone's looking the other way."

"And how do I do that?" asked James.

Mandy grinned. It was amazing how things fell into place when you were really determined. "Blackie," she said. "You know how much he likes feathers."

James looked at her. "Are you thinking what I think you're thinking?" he asked.

"Mrs. Ponsonby's hat," said Mandy.

James let out a whistle. "After that stuff with the cake and Pandora she'll skin us alive."

"But you'll do it?" asked Mandy.

James nodded.

"Okay," she said. "You get going. I'll try to look as if I'm just walking Prince, giving him some exercise."

"Wait a minute," James said. "Where are you going to take him?"

Mandy looked around the open field. There were

no hiding places, and if she tried to get him back to Animal Ark she would be seen. Susan would be looking for Prince soon, and James couldn't keep everyone's attention forever, not even with the help of Blackie.

Then her eyes lit on the perfect hiding place. "In there," she said. "In the church."

"The *church*?" asked James. "What on earth will Pastor Walters say?"

Mandy shook her head. "I don't care," she said. "I just don't want Prince to have to jump. As long as I can keep him hidden until it's over, that's all I care about."

"Right," said James. "You start walking him across, and I'll get Blackie to do his stuff."

Prince turned his head and blew softly on Mandy's cheek. She reached a hand up and laid her ear against his chest. Deep inside she could hear his breath. It sounded normal, but if she was right, that didn't mean a thing. It was only when he was near hay that he couldn't breathe properly.

"It's all right, boy," she said to him. "You aren't going to jump until Dad's seen you, no matter what."

The pony nuzzled her shoulder as if he understood. She began to walk him away from the jumping ring. James was running for the cake competition stand, Blackie at his heels and Toby trying to keep up. Susan had turned around. She was looking for Prince. Mandy urged Prince along. If she could get behind the belt of trees that fringed the churchyard she would have more chance of avoiding notice, but there was still a long way to go.

"Oh, James," she muttered to herself. "Hurry!"

Mandy could see Susan quite clearly. She was looking all around. Any moment now she would spot them and the game would be up. The loudspeaker crackled into life, announcing the start of the third group. Susan began to look more urgently.

"Oh, please hurry, James," Mandy muttered.

Then from the other side of the field came a long-drawn-out howling. Something large and black shot across the jumping ring and began to caper madly. Blackie! Mrs. Ponsonby's hat was firmly clasped between his teeth. A figure ran after it — James. He was closely followed by several others. In moments the ring was covered with people all trying to catch the Labrador. Blackie was turning and twisting, keeping one step ahead of everyone chasing him.

Mandy risked another glance at Susan. Her dad was there now. She and her parents had turned toward the commotion.

"*Now*," Mandy said to Prince, and she urged the little pony across the open space to the belt of trees. Sounds rose in the air behind her, but she ignored them. They were coming from the show ring. No one was looking in her direction.

As swiftly as she could she urged the pony on. She didn't want to hurry him too much, but they didn't have much time.

"Not far now, Prince," she whispered.

Behind them the loudspeaker began to bellow to people to clear the ring. And then the church was there, only yards away.

Mandy gave one more glance backward and drew Prince across the open space to the door. She laid a hand on the heavy handle of the door into the church porch, hoping that it would be open. For a moment she thought it was locked and her heart sank. Then the heavy ring turned in her hand and the door opened. Mandy urged Prince through into the cool dimness of the porch.

She closed the door behind them, then she went and laid a hand on Prince's flank. "There, boy," she said. "You're safe now. And you aren't going back — not until the jumping is over."

Prince whinnied and nuzzled Mandy's shoulder. She turned her face into his warm neck and laid her hand on his mane. "It's all right, Prince," she whispered. "Dad will be here soon. He'll know what to do."

She stroked a hand across his coat and felt his sides heave slightly under her fingers. He was sweating a little. But she had led him gently enough toward the church — or as gently as she had been able. His eyes seemed to be pleading with her, asking for help.

Mandy loosened his girth and took off his saddle. She looked round. She needed something to rub him down with. He was cooling rapidly now.

But the porch was empty. She tried the door into the church. Locked. Then she saw a cupboard in the corner. She tugged the door open. Buckets, brooms, and rags. They looked clean enough.

Quickly Mandy wadded up a pile of rags and began to rub Prince down, talking to him all the while, soothing him, making small reassuring noises. After a while she could feel him grow calmer. She worked on and on until he was warm. She breathed a sigh of relief. If she could just keep him here until Dad came back from Twyford. If she could let him rest . . .

There was a sound at the porch door and a grating noise as it opened. Mandy froze. She looked around wildly but there was nowhere else to hide. She put herself between the door and Prince.

A shadow fell across the floor of the porch as the

door opened. James poked his head inside. Mandy felt her breath come out in a great rush of relief.

"Oh, James, you did a terrific job. Thanks a lot."

"I thought you might need help," James said. He rested his hand on Prince's neck. "How is he?" he said.

Mandy shook her head. "He seems better now, but even a little exercise seems to distress him. What's happening outside?" she said. "Where's Susan?"

James's face fell. "She knows, Mandy. She says you've taken her pony. She told the race steward and they're looking for you. It's only a matter of time before they find us."

"They'll never look here," said Mandy. "They'd never think of looking for a pony on a church porch."

James didn't seem too sure. "Once they've looked everywhere else," he said. "I mean, where else is there to look?"

Mandy thought for a moment. "What about you?" she said to James. "Did anybody see you come this way?"

James shook his head. "Nobody was bothered about me," he said. "Not once I'd caught Blackie and made him give Mrs. Ponsonby her hat back. By that time Susan had everybody looking for the pony."

"You're sure no one saw you?" asked Mandy.

James shook his head. "Positive," he said.

Just then there came a scratching at the porch door.

Mandy jumped. "What's that?" she asked.

James went red. "Oh, no!" he said.

He went to the door and opened it. Blackie bounded in. He was carrying Mrs. Ponsonby's hat in his mouth.

James groaned. "Oh, no, Blackie," he said. "You didn't steal it again . . ." Then his voice trailed off.

"What is it?" Mandy asked.

James was looking toward Farmer Redpath's field. Mandy came to stand beside him. There was a small stream of people heading their way. Mrs. Ponsonby was among them. And at that moment Susan looked up — and saw Mandy. Susan turned to her father and pointed. Quickly Mandy hid behind the porch door, but she knew it was too late. Susan had seen her.

She looked at James. "She's coming, isn't she?" she said.

James nodded and turned to Mandy. "It looks like we're in an awful lot of trouble," he said.

Twelve

Mandy put her arm round Prince's neck, as if to protect him.

"We could make a run for it," said James.

Mandy shook her head. "That's just the point," she said. "We can't. We're here to stop Prince from running. I couldn't do that to him."

James looked miserable. "So what do we do when they come?"

Mandy's shoulders slumped. "Try to convince them there's something wrong with Prince," she said. "But they'll never believe me. Nobody believes me." There were tears in her eyes.

"I believe you," said James.

Blackie whined gently and came and laid Mrs. Ponsonby's hat at Mandy's feet. Even though she felt so terrible she couldn't help smiling.

"And Blackie believes you," said James.

Just then the porch door burst open and a crowd of people poured in. Toby was with them.

Everyone started shouting at once. Mandy could hardly think for the noise. Above all came the voice of Mrs. Ponsonby. "My hat!" she cried. "Look at my poor hat."

Mandy looked down at the crushed bundle of pink felt and feathers.

Then Susan said, "I told you she had taken Prince."

Mandy's head came up. "He isn't well," she said. "There's something wrong with him."

"Do you realize what you've done?" the race judge said angrily to Mandy.

Mandy took a deep breath. "Prince isn't fit to jump," she said.

The race judge looked at her, then at Prince. "I've already told you. He seems all right to me," he said.

"He's all right now," said Mandy "but —"

She didn't get any further. "Why are we wasting time?" Susan said to her father. "You can see for yourself that Prince is okay."

Mandy felt desperate. "There is something wrong with Prince," she said. "I know it."

"What?" said the race judge.

Suddenly Mandy felt her confidence draining away. What if she was wrong after all? But she couldn't take the risk. "I think it's SAD," she said loudly.

"It certainly is sad when a young woman behaves the way you have," said Mrs. Ponsonby.

"I didn't mean that," said Mandy.

"What did you mean, then?" asked the race judge.

Mandy drew herself up. "It's an illness called SAD. It's like asthma in people. The heaves. I think he's allergic to hay."

"That's three diseases already," said Mrs. Ponsonby.

The race judge looked exasperated. "You stole a pony," he said. "That's a pretty serious thing to do."

"It's serious for Prince," she said. "If I'm right about this, if you let him jump and he gets hay in his lungs he might die."

"*If* you're right," said Mrs. Ponsonby. "So you admit you might be wrong, do you? That's a change."

"If you'd only listen . . ." said Mandy. She looked around helplessly. Her eyes came to rest on Susan's father. He was the only one who hadn't said anything yet. He had a kind face and he didn't look angry, just puzzled.

"I don't know anything about horses," he said, "but if there's any doubt about the pony's health maybe we should get a vet to look at him."

"Her dad is a vet," said Susan. "So is her mom. That's why she thinks she knows it all."

Mrs. Ponsonby cut in. "She does think she knows it all," she said. "Why, she even told me how to look after my little Pandora."

"You aren't feeding her properly," Mandy shouted, unable to stop herself. It was the wrong thing to say.

"What did I tell you?" Mrs. Ponsonby said, turning to Susan's father. "Rude little girl. Interfering with people and their pets. How can you believe a little vandal like that? Standing there bold as brass with my hat." And she reached over and snatched up her hat.

Mandy looked at Mr. Collins. He was her last hope. But she knew she had lost.

"The pony looks all right to me," he said.

Mandy tried one last time. "He *looks* all right," she said, "but he isn't. I'm sure he isn't."

The race judge looked at his watch again. "Make up your mind," he said.

"If you could give us proof . . ." said Mr. Collins.

Mandy shook her head. "I don't have any proof," she said miserably.

The race judge opened the porch door. "What's it to be then?" he asked.

Mr. Collins took hold of Prince's bridle as Susan began to buckle on the saddle. "I'm sure your intentions were good," he said. "But if the race judge doesn't see anything wrong with Prince . . ." He hesitated. "Besides, his previous owners said the pony had always been healthy."

"That's just it," Mandy said. "It's his feeding and his stabling. It's all wrong. The stables where he lived before —"

She didn't get any further. Mr. Collins interrupted her. "Mrs. Jackson was delighted with the stables at The Beeches," he said.

"They're brand-new," said Susan. "Poor Prince was living in a lean-to before we bought him."

"But it was healthier for him," Mandy protested.

At that Mrs. Ponsonby drew herself up. "Really, it's too much," she said to Mr. Collins. "First I don't know how to feed a dog, then you don't know how to stable a horse. I won't listen to another word of this nonsense. A lean-to healthier than a proper stable? It's ridiculous." She looked around. "I suppose you would keep a pony on a porch," she said to Mandy.

It was the worst moment of Mandy's life. She watched dumbly as Susan led Prince out of the porch. The others walked on ahead. At the last moment Susan turned back. "You think I don't love Prince as much as you do," she said, "but I do — and I'm going to win with him because he's the best pony in the world."

Mandy stood there dumbly as they disappeared. Even Toby went with them. She had tried her best. Tried — and failed.

Mandy and James stood outside the church porch watching the small procession heading toward the ring. The loudspeaker announced that Barry Prescott had a faultless round. Mandy's heart turned over. That meant Susan had to win on time alone. It wouldn't be enough not to make any mistakes. She would have to push Prince to the limit.

"Oh, I wish Dad would come," Mandy said. "I keep thinking about Duke nearly dying. And he's a big, strong workhorse."

"Do you really think that might happen to Prince?" asked James. "Do you think he might collapse?"

Mandy nodded. "Even walking him this far made him breathless. And if he gets hay in his lungs from the jump —" Mandy stopped. She couldn't bear to think of it.

James nodded. "What's that?"

Mandy turned her head to the road behind them. A car was coming down the road toward the church, making for the turnoff into Farmer Redpath's field. She looked toward the jumping ring. Susan was up on Prince, trotting him around the field, ready to go into the ring. Mandy looked back toward the road. She could see the car more clearly now. She grabbed James's sleeve. "It's Dad," she said. "Stop him. Get him to come at once to the ring. I don't care what he says. Just get him there."

And then she was halfway down the path, running.

James's eyes were wide. "Where are you going?" he yelled.

Mandy turned as she ran. "To stop Prince from jumping," she called back. "Get Dad. I'll hold them up as long as I can."

As she ran she risked one last look back. James was on his way, flying toward the turnoff to stop the car. Blackie was like a shadow at his heels. She hoped he would make it — hoped he would be able to persuade her father that it was a matter of life or death.

Her feet pounded on the path. The breath rasped

in her throat but she paid no attention. Her eyes were fixed on the ring. She saw Susan bring Prince up to the start, waiting for the signal to begin her round.

Mandy reached the belt of trees and crashed through them, not caring about the scratches she got from branches. She was nearly there. Only a few more yards to go.

Susan had started her canter around the ring, and then she would start the jumps. Mandy increased her pace. Suddenly she felt her foot catch in a tree root. She went over, tumbling heavily to the ground. The impact of her fall knocked the breath out of her body.

She struggled up and began to run again. There was a searing pain in her ankle and she felt weak in her stomach. She looked toward the ring. Susan was gathering the reins, urging Prince into a gallop.

Mandy tested the weight on her left foot. It was agony. She gritted her teeth. Running, hobbling, ignoring the pain, she made her way through the rest of the trees and into the ring. All she could think of was Prince. He mustn't gallop. She repeated it to herself, trying to blot out the pain in her foot. *He mustn't gallop. He mustn't jump.* She was running down the middle of the ring now, running straight for Prince.

"Stop!" she cried. "You have to stop!"

Mandy could see the race judge running out on to the field. She could see the faces of the other riders looking at her in shock. She could see Susan's face turned to her in disbelief.

She made one last effort. The pain in her foot was almost blinding her now. Gathering her strength, she ran on past the five-bar gate, past the hay bales. Prince recognized her and threw his head up, whinnying. Susan let the reins drop and he slowed, breathing heavily.

Mandy reached him and threw an arm around his neck. Susan looked down at her. "What are you doing?" she said angrily. "You've ruined everything."

Mandy could hardly speak. She was out of breath, and the pain in her foot was coming in waves now. Around her people had started to gather, people shouting, asking questions, demanding what she was up to. Some of the riders had dismounted and were coming toward her, leading their ponies.

But she had stopped Susan and Prince! Mandy didn't care what they would do to her. She didn't care that they were shouting at her. She only cared about Prince. He wouldn't have to jump now.

The race judge stood in front of her, his face red with anger. "This is going too far . . ." he began.

Mandy leaned against Prince for support, trying to gather her strength.

Then another voice spoke, a voice she knew and trusted. "What's the trouble?" asked Dr. Adam. "Mandy? Are you all right?"

Mandy turned to her father in relief. James was beside him, grinning. "You did it, Mandy!" he said.

Mandy managed a smile before she said to her father, "It's Prince, Dad. You can't let him jump."

And then, in front of them all, she slid down the pony's flank and fainted.

Thirteen

"We'll have to issue tickets soon, you're getting so many visitors," Dr. Adam joked.

Mandy looked up at him. It was the Thursday after the Welford County Fair, and she was sitting in a deck chair in the sunny garden behind Animal Ark, her leg propped up on a stool. Her foot was still swathed in an elastic bandage but the swelling wasn't nearly as bad now.

"Hello, Mr. Pickard," she said as Walter came up the path. Tommy was with him, holding his cage of hamsters. "Not more chewing gum, Tommy?" she said.

Tommy blushed. "I brought them to see you," he

said, holding out the cage. "They won a prize at the show."

"The prize for the most unusual appearance," said Dr. Adam. "I donated the prize myself."

Walter chuckled, but Tommy was clearly proud of his prize. "It was a jumbo pack of chewing gum," he said. "Just for me."

Mandy looked at the little animals. They still looked a bit odd but their fur was beginning to grow back.

"How's the invalid?" asked Walter.

Mandy smiled. "I'm fine," she said. "But people are making a terrible fuss over me."

"We can't move for all the get-well cards, and the house has more flowers in it than the garden does," said Dr. Adam.

This time it was Mandy's turn to blush. She hadn't realized how popular she was. Every day had brought more visitors.

On Sunday it had been Kate and Melanie. "A week off school," Melanie said. "Lucky you!"

"She nearly had to break her ankle for it," Kate said. "I didn't know you hated school that much, Mandy."

Mandy smiled at the thought as she played with Tommy's hamsters, while Dad and Walter had a talk about Mom's roses and Tommy went into the house for some lemonade. Her ankle hadn't been broken, just very badly sprained.

"You were lucky there," Dr. Prescott had said. "But you'll have to keep it up for a week."

"Try some of your dad's liniment," Barry had said when he came on Monday. "It worked like magic for Star." Mandy nearly took him seriously till she saw the glint in his eyes. "Anyway," he said, "I thought what you did was great."

Mandy tickled one of the hamsters under the chin and remembered how she had come out of that faint and had looked at Prince safe in Dad's care. She would gladly have broken an ankle for Prince's sake.

Then there was Grandma and Grandpa and the McFarlanes and Betty Hilder and the Mabsons and Penny Hapwell and her mom with Cally and the Metcalfs and Mr. Hardy — the list was endless. Even Dan Venables came to see her.

"You saved that pony's life," he said when Dr. Emily brought him in.

Mandy had looked at him in alarm. "Was it really as bad as that?"

Dan looked at Dr. Emily. "You'd have to ask the expert," he said. "But I figure you did."

"There was a lot of dust in Prince's airways," said Dr. Emily. "Hay dust mostly, but fine sawdust as well, and mold spores from his bedding. If he had been forced to jump there's no telling what might have happened. He had been in that stable all day Friday. He was pretty weak in the chest by Saturday. If he had been pushed too hard, he could have been harmed for life."

"So I did the right thing, Mom?" said Mandy.

Dr. Emily nodded. "Oh, yes, Mandy, you did the right thing. Everybody knows that now."

Two of the nicest visitors were Jane and Mrs. Jackson.

"Prince never had any trouble with his chest when we owned him," Mrs. Jackson said.

"That's because we kept him in the open most of the time, Mom," Jane said. "And we fed him lots of oats and bran and let him graze in the orchard."

"Dad always said there wasn't a better looked-after pony in the area," said Mandy.

"He'll be all right now, won't he?" said Mrs. Jackson. "If they aren't looking after him properly I'll go right over there and bring him home."

Mandy laughed. Little Mrs. Jackson looked so fierce. "You don't have to do that," she said. "Dad has seen to all that. He says Susan has a bedroom full of books on how to look after ponies now, and her mom is helping her."

That was another thing. Susan's mom hadn't

gone back to London right away. She had stayed at The Beeches.

"Susan says her mom and dad are talking about her mom doing less TV work and spending more time with her," James said on one of his daily visits.

Mandy bit her lip. "Susan hasn't come to see me," she said. "I mean her mom and dad sent this great big basket of flowers . . ."

"She's too embarrassed," James said. "She says she can't face you, she feels so awful."

Mandy looked up, surprised. "That's crazy," she said. "How was she to know? She doesn't know anything about horses, apart from how to ride them."

"She's trying to learn," James said

Mandy grew thoughtful. Maybe Susan was changing. Then she thought of something else. "James," she said. "What happened to Toby?"

James shuffled. "He has a new home," he said. "He's really happy there." James sounded surprised.

"That's what Mom and Dad say," said Mandy. "But they won't tell me where he is."

"I'd better go," said James. And Mandy just knew he was hiding something from her.

But now it was Thursday, and Susan still hadn't come to see her. Mandy dozed in the deck chair.

The sun was warm, and she felt her eyes closing. Vaguely she heard sounds. A kind of *clip-clop*, like a pony coming up the path.

Her eyes flew open. It *was* a pony. It was Prince — and he looked wonderful. His coat gleamed, his eyes were bright, and he whinnied and tried to pull away from Susan.

Susan let the leading rein go and Prince made his way delicately across the grass, bent his head and nuzzled Mandy's ear. He blew gently and her hair lifted. "That tickles," she said to him, reaching up to stroke his nose. "Oh, Prince, I'm so glad to see you."

"He's all right now," said Susan. "He really is. Your dad says so."

Mandy looked at Susan standing there, awkward, near to tears. "I'm so sorry, Mandy," she said. "I should have listened to you. I nearly killed Prince. I don't know what to say."

Mandy smiled. "Everything is okay now," she said and saw Susan's shoulders sag with relief.

"And you'll help me to look after him?" said Susan.

Mandy laughed. "Just try to keep me away," she said.

Behind Susan she could see Mr. and Mrs. Collins coming up the path. Prince moved away and began to crop the short grass of the lawn.

"We might have to get another horse soon," said Susan's dad, smiling at his wife.

"If I can get away more often," Mrs. Collins said. "I'm going to try and cut down on work."

"And so am I," said Mr. Collins. "Susan will soon be complaining that she can't get rid of us."

But when Mandy looked at Susan's happy face she didn't think that would be a problem. Susan looked really content and much more at home. Mandy thought she might have found a new friend.

The garden gate swung open again just as Mandy's parents came out of the house. It was

James and Blackie and behind them was someone else: Mrs. Ponsonby. But something was different. She was still wearing the pink hat. It was a bit crushed but it still had its feathers.

For a moment Mandy couldn't figure out what had changed. Then she realized Mrs. Ponsonby wasn't carrying Pandora. Mandy looked down. There was Pandora waddling up the path, and by her side — Toby!

"See why we didn't tell you before," Dr. Adam said to Mandy. "Mrs. Ponsonby decided to adopt him. We didn't think you'd be able to stand the shock."

Mrs. Ponsonby sailed up the path. In her hands she carried an enormous box of chocolates tied up with a yellow ribbon. "My dear, brave child," she said, "what you did was a lesson to us all. Risking yourself for that sweet little pony as you did. Such courage. I was saying to your grandmother only to-day how proud she must be of you."

Mandy just gaped while Mrs. Ponsonby went on about her being an example to other young people. Pandora and Toby played happily at her feet. Pandora even managed a little run — almost. Was it Mandy's imagination or had Pandora slimmed down a bit?

Blackie came and plonked himself down beside

Mandy and started licking her face. Then Mrs. Ponsonby presented the chocolates to her with a flourish and bent to kiss her cheek. If it hadn't been for her ankle, Mandy would have tried to run away. As it was she had to grab Blackie's collar as the feathers came within reach.

"Don't eat them all at once," Mrs. Ponsonby said, straightening up. "After all, too many chocolates aren't good for you. I don't give my precious Pandora or Toby anything like that. Aren't they wonderful together? They have such fun, and Pandora really is becoming quite lively."

Mandy looked around. The garden was full to bursting with people and animals. Mom and Dad, Susan and her parents, James, Mrs. Ponsonby, Blackie and Toby and Pandora. There was one animal missing, though. "Where's Prince?" she asked.

James's eyes opened wide. "On the porch," he said, "eating the geraniums."

"Oh, that's all right then," said Mandy.

"Is it?" said Mr. Collins. "I mean, the porch?"

Mrs. Ponsonby turned to him majestically. "Mr. Collins," she said, "if Mandy says a pony on the porch is all right, then a pony on the porch is all right."

And then everybody laughed — even Mrs. Ponsonby.

LOOK FOR

PUPPIES in the PANTRY

by Ben M. Baglio

The next morning Mandy jumped out of bed. The garden sparkled in the morning sun. There had been a storm in the night. Mandy had woken once to a tremendous crack of thunder.

She had a tight knot of excitement in her stomach. If she was lucky George Sims would call from Bleakfell Hall today to say the horses had arrived. She would get to see Charley and Mr. Baggins again!

Mandy felt restless. She had her chores to do in the office but couldn't seem to settle down to anything. Luckily, the call from Bleakfell Hall came just a few minutes later.

"The horses have arrived," Dr. Emily said, popping her head around the door.

"Great!" Mandy said excitedly, full of energy all of a sudden. "I'll call James."

James arrived on his bike just as they were getting in the car. Mandy could see he had rushed. His sweatshirt was on backwards, but she figured she'd wait to tell him.

Jess climbed onto James's lap, curled up, and fell asleep right away.

When they arrived at Bleakfell Hall they could hear a lot of shouting from inside.

They left Jess curled up in the back of the car, making sure to leave the windows open.

"Maybe we'd better go around to the yard," Dr. Emily suggested. "It sounds as if they're pretty busy in there. I know where the stables are."

"Let's go and find Charley," Mandy said to James.

There was no answer to their knock on the back door. Cautiously, Mandy opened it and poked her head around.

"Hello . . . anybody here?" She turned to James. "Come on, I'm sure they won't mind if we go in."

The vast kitchen was empty. No Charley, no Mr. Baggins, no cats, no George Sims. Where on earth was everyone?

The sound of Mr. Curtis's voice came echoing along the passage that led to the great hallway.

Mandy pulled James's sleeve. "Come on, let's take a look. Maybe all the animals are on the set."

They crept along the corridor and peered around the half-open door.

The place was in an uproar.

Mandy stifled a giggle. "I told you it was chaotic," she whispered to James.

Ben sat on top of a stepladder, waving his arms about. The ladder wobbled. Someone rushed forward to steady it. Mandy put her hand over her mouth to stop the laughter coming out.

"No!" Mr. Curtis was shouting. "Not there, for goodness' sake, someone get hold of that parrot!"

A woman in an ankle-length white dress was sitting by the fireplace. There was a blanket over her head. The cats were asleep on the sofa as if nothing was going on.

"That must be Antonia Kent," Mandy whispered in James's ear. "She's the human star."

"I'm not acting with that horrible bird!" a voice came from under the blanket. "I'm not, I'm not, I'm not!"

"Look!" Mandy said, suddenly spying the parrot. "There's Mr. Baggins!"

Sure enough, high up on the elegant crystal chandelier, Mr. Baggins preened his feathers. Beneath, an assistant held up a cup of sunflower seeds.

"Come down, Mr. Baggins," she was shouting. "Nice dinner."

"Two sugars!" the parrot screeched. *"A cup of Baggins if you please."*

Mandy was laughing so hard she felt sure someone would hear.

"Where's George Sims?" Mr. Curtis yelled suddenly. "He's supposed to be supervising these wretched creatures."

"What a mess," James whispered.

"We'd better get out of here before we get in trouble," Mandy said.

But it was too late. They had been spotted.

"Ah, young lady," Mr. Curtis called. "Come in, come in. Any hope of you getting that bird to come down?"

Mandy and James sidled into the hall. Mandy looked up. "I'll try," she said. She felt a bit shy in front of all the crew. "But I can't promise."

Across the hall, Antonia Kent peeped out from under her blanket. Mandy almost laughed again. The actress looked like a nun in a cocktail dress with the white blanket around her face. But when she took the blanket off, Mandy drew in her breath. She recognized her right away. Antonia Kent was the heroine of one of Mandy's favorite soap operas! She just couldn't help staring.

"Mandy . . ." James nudged her in the ribs.

"Oh!" Mandy shook herself. She stood under the chandelier. "Mr. Baggins," she called softly. "Come on down, Mr. Baggins. You're being very naughty."

"She loves, you, yeah, yeah, yeah," Mr. Baggins said.

"Yes," Mandy couldn't help grinning. "I know, but please come down, huh?"

Mandy heard laughter echoing around the set. She glanced at Mr. Curtis. He had a face like thunder. He definitely didn't think it was funny, even if everyone else did.

Mandy pursed her lips. She pretended to frown. "Now come on, Mr. Baggins, stop fooling around." Someone passed her the cup of sunflowers seeds and she held them out. "Come on . . . please."

To Mandy's relief, Mr. Baggins cocked his head on one side, spread his bright wings, and fluttered down toward her. He landed on her head. Mandy tottered. Then she caught sight of herself in a big, gold-framed wall mirror. She looked as if she was wearing a gaily colored hat in an Easter parade.

She put her hand up. "Come on, you rotten thing. You're holding everyone up."

Mr. Baggins stepped daintily onto her fingers. A sigh of relief washed around the room.

"Well *done*, darling." Antonia Kent swept toward Mandy in a wave of pale silk and strong perfume. She had black hair tied up in curls on top of her head, and a pale complexion with a dark beauty spot on her rouged cheek. The actress eyed the parrot warily as she put her arm around Mandy's shoulders. "This girl has a magic touch." She turned to the crew. "Is she the new animal trainer? Has that hopeless man gone at last?"

Mr. Curtis walked over. "No," he said. "She's the vet's daughter. That was terrific, Mandy. Maybe you could stay and help out? We need Charley next. Could you get her?"

"Oh, yes." Mandy's heart leaped with excitement. "I'd love to."

Just then the front door opened and George Sims came through into the hall. He looked upset. His green boots were covered with mud. His face was red, as if he had been running.

"Sims," Mr. Curtis said, "I was just sending Mandy to get the dog."

George Sims bit his lip. "The dog's gone," he said

gruffly, looking down at the toes of his boots. "She ran off."

"What!" Mr. Curtis groaned.

Mandy's stomach turned icy with fear. "Oh, no!" she cried. "When?"

Make a Home for Someone You Love!

ANIMAL ARK

Meet Mandy and her best friend, James—two kids who do everything they can to help pets in trouble!

Animal Ark #1: **Kittens in the Kitchen**

Animal Ark #2: **Pony on the Porch**

Animal Ark #3: **Puppies in the Pantry**

Animal Ark #4: **Goat in the Garden**

A Note About Animals from the ASPCA

The ASPCA is the American Society for the Prevention of Cruelty to Animals. Our organization started working to protect animals more than 130 years ago! This book tells an interesting story about how Mandy and her friends prevented a pony from being injured. Ponies and horses have a long history of living with people, both for work and pleasure. Here are some things you should remember about them:

- Horses and ponies can be wonderful companion animals, but they grow very large and can often require more time and money to care for than the usual cat, dog or guinea pig.

- Horses and ponies can work and play very hard, but they also need rest and care. They should never be forced to race or show if they are sick or tired.

- If you see an animal that looks like it is being treated badly or unfairly, tell an adult about the problem and see what can be done to help the animal.

- In this book, Mandy is very lucky that her parents are animal doctors and can help her. In real life, animals can also get help from animal shelters, nature centers, park rangers, wildlife rehabilitators, obedience trainers, and local humane organizations.

(more on back)

Some Special News About the ASPCA's Junior Membership Club: ASPCA Animaland

Now you can help the ASPCA protect animals by becoming a member of ASPCA Animaland. Have fun learning facts about animals, as well as how important it is to respect all living things in our environment! Animaland membership includes an exciting and colorful bi-monthly magazine, official membership card and club pin, member's activity guidebook, and a welcome letter from ASPCA president Roger A. Caras.

For more information, write us at ASPCA Animaland, 424 East 92nd St., New York, NY 10128 or e-mail us at animaland@aspca.org.